BEAUTY AND HIS BEAST

BEY DECKARD

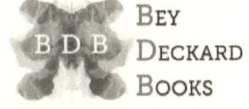

BEY
DECKARD
BOOKS

CONTENTS

Author's Note   vii

1. Juniper Bo   1
2. Captain Marrex   9
3. The Stellerion   15
4. The Hidden Garden   21
5. Juniper Screws Up   27
6. The Accident   37
7. Making Changes   45
8. Dinner, Dinner?   53
9. Confessions   69
10. Cut to the Chase   89
11. Calling Home   95
12. Terra Deux   105
13. Stimulation and Interference   119
14. Sabotage   129
15. Walking into a Dream   137
    Epilogue – 3 Months Later   145

    Books by Bey Deckard   151
    About the Author   153

ISBN (D2D): 978-1-989250-09-9
ISBN (Amazon): 978-0-9947900-9-5

I'd like to thank all my readers. Your enthusiastic support means the world to me.

Thank you to Starr... you are my sunshine.

And, a special thank you to Riina for letting me use her rose picture on the cover! xo

AUTHOR'S NOTE

TL;DR - THIS STORY IS BASED ON THE ORIGINAL CLASSIC, NOT THE DISNEY VERSION.

Once upon a time, long long ago, someone gave me an illustrated copy of *Beauty and the Beast* as a present. The story was a retelling of a retelling: this was Deborah Apy's version retelling the one written by Jeanne-Marie Leprince de Beaumont in 1756, which was a retelling of the original story, *La Belle et la Bête* written by Gabrielle-Suzanne Barbot de Villeneuve in 1740. I loved the story and the illustrations by Michael Hague really intrigued me—they were creepy, dark, and fantastic. I loved his images of the horned, shaggy-albeit-well-dressed, angst-ridden Beast. Interestingly, we never get to see the miraculous transformation of the prince... The final painting in the book is of Beauty finding the Beast dying of heartbreak in his rose garden.

Years later, I would see the Disney version and though the story isn't all that similar to the original, I liked the comedic aspects of it. However, I was disappointed with the Beast's transformation—call me strange, but I actually preferred him as he was.

Beauty and His Beast is a story that's been percolating in my brain for a few years now. It's a mashup of the original stories, the Disney version, and a bit of another book that has *nothing* to do with *Beauty and the Beast*, but was my *absolute* favourite when I was really young: Disney's *The Black Hole: A Spaceship Adventure for Robots*.

This story is not dark, not very long, and not particularly serious—just my silly take on a much-loved, oft-retold fairy tale... in space.

I hope you enjoy it.

P.S. - Ghelyxian is pronounced Hell-EE-zee-an, and Ghelyx, Hell-ix

CHAPTER I
JUNIPER BO

S cowling, Marrex tapped the dust-covered panel, and the green light flickered faintly. There was no doubt about it —the stasis pod was still powered, if only barely. That meant whoever was inside might be alive. Marrex stepped back and crossed his arms, not happy about the situation.

"Sir?" VAL's perfect oval face appeared in the air in front of Marrex, soft dove-grey and smooth like glass. "Are you going to open it? You're not just going to let them die, are you?"

Marrex grunted, staring at the etched nameplate on the pod. *Juniper Bo.*

"Captain?"

Marrex swatted at the AI's holoprojection, making it waver and retreat by half a meter—VAL's blank round eyes contemplated the captain for a moment before he tried again. "There is a *person* in there, Captain."

"So?" Marrex snorted and shook his great furry head in irritation.

"So, you have an obligation to try to save them... don't you?" VAL replied.

"And have a stranger on my ship?"

"Well... *yes*," the AI said, his face going pale pink. "But is that *such* a bad thing, sir? You'd have company..."

Marrex grunted again and turned around, climbing down out of the small wreck, and the holoprojection followed him.

"You're just going to blow the pod out the airlock, then?" VAL's tone was reproachful.

"Didn't say that," muttered Marrex. He lengthened his strides, and VAL's image wobbled with the effort of keeping up. The captain smacked the button next to the doors and left the shuttlebay, taking the long main corridor that ran the entire length of the *Stellerion*.

"But... Captain? You should do something *soon*. That power cell is nearly depleted. It's amazing it's still working as it is..."

"It can wait!" Marrex hadn't meant to shout, but the AI was testing his patience. "Where's S1N?"

"Right here," said the second holoprojection as it appeared. Unlike VAL who had a humanoid face, S1N resembled something the ship's database called a "cat," a black four-legged furry creature with huge yellow-green eyes. Despite Marrex's best efforts to change the holoprojection, he seemed to be stuck with the silly thing.

"I'm hungry," Marrex growled.

S1N paused in his tongue bath, looking up to appraise the captain with narrowed eyes. "When are you *not*?" The cat's mouth didn't move when it spoke in its perpetually bored tone.

"Send something to my quarters. Not whatever it was I had this morning. Something that has actual taste."

The cat pitched himself on his side and yawned wide, showing his white fangs and pink tongue. "Something with taste. Got it." S1N pawed at the air, his sharp claws curling out and retracting. "So... VAL says you're going to murder someone."

"That wasn't what I said," replied VAL, turning a deeper shade of pink.

"You *distinctly* said if he doesn't do something to help that poor pod person, it's as good as murder."

"Well—"

"Food. *Now!*" Marrex roared and bashed the side of his fist against the metal bulkhead, sending a reverberating *gonggg* down the corridor. Both AIs winked out simultaneously.

A FEW HOURS LATER, S1N found an old service droid tottering through the shuttlebay. "What are you doing with that thing?" he asked, tail swishing behind him as he walked along in midair.

VAL's voice came from the small speaker in the droid's side. The AI didn't have enough processing power to project his image *and* control the droid while simultaneously taking care of his primary function, which was life support aboard the colossal Chato-class starship.

"Nothing that should concern you," VAL said, sounding flustered.

Because of the way the firewall was configured between their two independent systems, the AIs were forced to communicate the old-fashioned way like a couple of meat-bags, but S1N didn't really mind—inflection had its merits. He pranced along beside the droid. "You're going to go wake up that Human, aren't you?"

"Human? How do you know it's a Human?" VAL replied.

The rear wheel of the old service droid squeaked rhythmically, and S1N amused himself by stepping in time to it. "Easy. I patched into the shuttle's computer. It was damaged, but I found out that there is one Human in stasis and one missing Nelami pilot who probably got sucked out into the black when the ship hit the asteroid."

"Did the captain ask you to check that?" The service droid stopped moving, and S1N walked a lazy circle around it.

"Yes, he did."

"Does that mean he's not going to let the Human die?"

"Didn't say that, did I? Maybe he was just curious. I wouldn't hold out for a happy rescue... you *know* how he can be," S1N said. He stopped walking and hovered in front of the droid, batting at its bent antenna. "And if you wake up the Human without permission, the captain's going to wipe you."

With a buzz and a squeak, the droid bumbled forward again on its warped wheels, passing through S1N's holoprojection.

"Rude!" said the cat, reappearing in front of the scavenged shuttlecraft. He watched VAL extend the droid's clamps to either side of the hatch.

"You're not trying to stop me," VAL pointed out as the service droid started pulling itself up into the small ship.

"It's your funeral. Why should I care if you're wiped? I'm tired of you anyway."

VAL stopped again. Despite the facelessness of the squat metal droid, it somehow managed to convey worry.

"You really think he'd wipe me?" VAL asked in a quiet voice.

"I don't think he *wouldn't* wipe you," S1N replied coolly.

For a few seconds, the VAL droid just sat there, then it continued pulling itself into the open hatch. "I don't care," he said. "I can't just stand back and do nothing. And he didn't specifically order *me* not to open the pod."

"Suit yourself." Yawning, S1N stretched out on the damaged control panel to watch VAL use the droid's front claw to work the mechanism on the stasis pod. Despite his studied nonchalance, S1N's curiosity was piqued. Besides, VAL was sure to bungle something up and then S1N would *have* to help him out; he patched into the shuttle's computer again just in case.

After some difficulty, the repair droid managed to press the correct key sequence, and an alarm bleated a deafening warning in the cramped space.

"Oh, darn it," VAL swore as he banged the claw against the front of the pod, trying to silence the noise.

With a twitch of his tail, S1N easily turned off the pod's decompression alarm, blinking sleepily at the droid.

"See? There we go," VAL said, completely oblivious to S1N's help. "I have this under control."

"Mmhmm."

A moment later, the pod's seam parted with a hiss, filling the shuttle with a cool mist. The lights on the panel went amber, then back to green as the mist dissipated, revealing the pod's occupant. Ears pricked forward, S1N sat up, peering at the figure.

"Oh, my goodness," he said, his tail swishing behind him. Within the stasis pod was a young adult Human male, with creamy pale skin and a mane of rich chestnut hair surrounding an exquisitely beautiful face.

"What? What's wrong?" asked VAL, obviously alarmed by S1N's reaction. "Is it dead?"

"He's not dead," S1N replied as he leapt into the air to hover in front of the young man. "But he *is* drop-dead gorgeous."

Slowly, the young man's lids lifted, revealing a pair of dark-brown eyes threaded through with lines of gold.

"How can you tell?" VAL asked.

S1N snorted with amusement and shook his head. "You have an overactive morality chip yet no sense of aesthetics at all."

"Where... am I?" said the Human, his voice deeper than S1N expected, an interesting juxtaposition to his almost ethereal beauty.

"You are aboard the *Stellerion*. Currently, we are passing through the aBi nebula outside the Omatrem system in the Frex Symio Frex Ha galaxy," S1N replied primly. Navigation was his primary function when he wasn't arranging the captain's meals with the fussy replicators.

"The... Frex... what?" the young man replied, rubbing his face. "How did I get here?"

"Your shuttle was damaged in an asteroid collision. We found it drifting and brought it aboard," VAL said. "Are you Juniper Bo?"

JUNIPER blinked at the talking trash can, then focused on the floating black cat again. What kind of messed-up dream was he having? "Yeah. That's me," he said and tried to step out of the stasis pod. He grabbed quickly onto the side of it, his legs strangely wobbly. Memories started flooding back—maybe it wasn't a dream after all. Had he arrived on Rhesh-14?

"How long have I been asleep?"

"One thousand years," the black cat replied in a slow, sonorous voice, its yellow-green eyes wide.

The words made Juniper's stomach plunge down through the decking, his pulse racing. *"What?"*

A bright-blue face, glassy smooth and subtly transparent, appeared next to the cat.

"Why would you *say* that?" It turned to Juniper. "Don't listen to him," said the face, its round eyes darting to the side. "There's something wrong with his empathy subroutine." It focused on Juniper again, its colour shifting to violet. "I am VAL. What is the last thing you remember, Juniper?"

"I... remember getting into the stasis pod and the technician telling me to look at a light."

"When and where was this?" the floating face asked kindly.

Juniper felt like his mind was operating at half the speed it normally did. "Uh... aboard a colony ship at the Terra Deux spaceport... in the Elequen system. Uhh..." He scratched his head, dizzy and disoriented. "The year 426. And um... it was February?"

VAL smiled. "According to my calculations, that would mean you've only been asleep for seventeen of your Terran years."

The cat daintily licked its paw with a pink tongue. "So, I was off by a little bit." Then the floating feline sat straight up, his ears quivering. "Oh crap. The captain's awake."

"The captain?" Juniper asked, trying his legs again.

"Yes, please keep up. You're on a ship. There's a captain. I have to go." The cat winked out, and Juniper stared at the space where it had hung a moment earlier.

"What *is* that?"

"That is my counterpart, S1N. Together, we are the ship's computer."

"Sin?"

"Yes, but with a one: S-1-N. Can you walk?" VAL asked. "We really must get you to your quarters."

"My... quarters?"

CHAPTER 2
CAPTAIN MARREX

Juniper sat on the edge of the bed, still feeling jittery from the long slow walk from the shuttlebay to his new quarters. The two AIs had taken turns escorting him while the other was off doing something for this mysterious captain. From the way they were acting, Juniper gathered they weren't telling him something.

Clearing his throat, he looked around the empty room. "VAL?" he said quietly. A second later, VAL's smooth orange face appeared in midair, and to his surprise, S1N slinked out from under the bed.

"Don't want to sleep?" VAL asked, and then it frowned. "Though I suppose you wouldn't, come to think of it."

"Sorry, I was just wondering if I could have something to eat," Juniper replied. "And maybe something to wear?" He looked down at the white stasis suit he wore with its trailing wires and tubes.

"Oh! Of course!" VAL replied, drifting to a section of wall that slid open at his approach. "Take a look in here, and see if you can find something suitable. If not, I'm sure we can find something in another room."

"Thank you," Juniper said, looking at the selection of

clothing. Most of it appeared at least humanoid, if not entirely to his tastes. "And some food?"

S1N had been chasing something only he could see, darting back and forth across the short-pile grey carpeting, but at Juniper's words, he came to a rigid stop, his ears pricked up and tail lashing. "I'm afraid you'll have to wait a little longer. The captain is up and about."

"Why can't I meet him?" Juniper asked, pulling out a pair of dark-blue pants that looked his size. "Aren't captains supposed to greet new passengers? Isn't that how it's done?"

The AIs started simultaneously.

"Well, yes, but—"

"It's—" They stopped, just staring at him.

"What? Is he too busy? Too important?" he asked, unzipping his stasis suit. "Antisocial?" Glancing over his shoulder at the holoprojected AIs, he saw them share a look. Juniper laughed, feeling uneasy. "What aren't you telling me?"

"Erm…" VAL's projected face went from orange to a sickly green, and S1N looked away, scratching at an itch, but the end of his tail was flicking rapidly.

"He doesn't know I'm awake, does he?" Juniper guessed, cinching the pants at the waist.

"No," VAL and S1N said together.

Juniper frowned, looking for a shirt and seeing nothing he liked. "Why not?"

"Captain Marrex preferred you as a Human-popsicle," said S1N, sharpening his claws on the carpet.

Juniper stared at the cat, nervously wondering what sort of situation he had landed in.

"The captain is a… complicated man," VAL said, his face becoming a pale lemon-yellow. "I'm certain he would have woken you up… eventually."

"That sounds ominous," Juniper joked, but when neither AI said anything, his heart did a quick double-beat that stole his breath. "Wait, he wasn't just going to let me *die* in there, was he? You said the pod was down to its last fuel cell."

"You see... the captain is a bit of a... um, solitary person," VAL said, the yellow of his face getting even paler.

"He's a real grump," S1N added. "Terrible temper."

"He's... not going to do anything *bad* to me, is he?" Juniper asked.

"No, he is not," replied a deep gravelly voice. "The captain simply doesn't like unexpected visitors."

Turning slowly, Juniper looked up at the hulking creature in the doorway and felt as if his heart had stopped completely. The beast had four wickedly sharp–looking black horns that twisted and curved around a wide face covered in blood-red fur. Black, pupilless eyes stared at Juniper from above a blunt snout filled with sharp yellow teeth. The creature was dressed in the black uniform of an Imperial captain, with gold-trimmed epaulettes and a double line of gold buttons down the front, and from the beast's wide shoulders hung a dark-red floor-length cape that nearly matched its fur.

With brawny arms crossed over its barrel chest, it stared hard at Juniper. Then, extending one four-fingered hand, it pointed a long hooked claw at VAL.

"I'll want a word with *you*, later," the beast growled. "*Leave us.*"

"Yes, Captain," VAL said, vanishing.

"You too, S1N."

The black cat gave Juniper a wide-eyed, somewhat apprehensive look and disappeared.

Marrex contemplated the young man standing half-naked in front of him. The moment he'd woken up and found the ship's AIs slow to respond to his queries, he'd known they were up to something, but he never thought they'd go so far in their disobedience. Certainly, it was VAL behind waking the Human because it wasn't like S1N to do anything charitable on his own —maybe it was time to wipe *both* their databanks clean and start fresh. *Maybe.*

In truth, Marrex had been planning on opening the pod himself after he'd gotten some sleep—he wasn't heartless, after all. However, now that he was face-to-face with one of the most beautiful creatures he'd ever seen, he didn't know which he regretted more: not waking the young man himself earlier or bringing him on board to begin with.

The young man was tall with fair skin, lean muscles, and a head of thick dark hair falling past his perfect dusky-pink nipples. His jaw was angular and chin square, but these sharp edges were offset by a wide mouth with plump, shapely lips that were parted with his rapid breathing. His narrow nose had a slightly crooked bridge that gave his face something far more alluring than symmetry, but the best came last as Marrex met the young man's wide gaze: large dark eyes that were gilded in gold and trimmed with long lashes—beautiful eyes full of fear tempered by lively curiosity.

"Thank you, sir, for allowing me onto your ship," said the young man in a velvety soft voice. "My name is Juniper Bo."

"I'm Captain Marrex," the captain replied gruffly, letting his eyes linger on the way Juniper's rib cage heaved, his abdomen tense. Obviously, the young man was trying to control his breathing to seem more confident, but all it did was give away how nervous he was... while drawing attention to the beautiful definition of his muscles. "Until I find you something useful to do, you're to remain in your quarters."

Juniper's chin lifted, his gaze narrowing. He took a step forward. "I'm a prisoner?"

"You're an *unwelcome* guest for the time being," Marrex replied, looking away. He couldn't stand seeing his ugliness reflected in the young man's eyes. "You'll only get in the way."

"Why not drop me off at the nearest port? Or planet?"

"Not possible. Not yet." Scowling, Marrex turned to leave. "Now, just stay out of my way."

"But why not? Surely—"

"*No*," Marrex snarled over his shoulder. He bared his fangs at Juniper and was pleased when the young man stepped back, his eyes round with fright. Satisfied that he'd made an impression, Marrex closed the door and keyed in a lock code. He was in no mood to discuss his circumstances with anyone, no matter how pretty they were to look at.

"To me," he said as he tramped down the corridor towards the bridge. Instantly, VAL and S1N were at his side.

"I'm sorry I took initiative, sir," VAL said in a meek voice. "I just felt like—"

"You're a machine. *You don't feel*," Marrex growled.

"What's your excuse, then?" S1N said, hovering next to his ear. "Did you have to yell at the poor kid? He's been asleep a long time, probably separated from his family, alone and confused and just looking for a friendly face—"

Marrex snorted and tossed his head, shearing harmlessly through the holoprojection with one of his horns, and S1N yowled, his fur standing on end.

"Marrex the Monster indeed," S1N hissed. "Sneaking around like a coward in his big old empty ship. Alone with his self-pity... mean and ugly and—"

"Go!" Marrex shouted, thoroughly sick of S1N's insolence.

"Gladly, asshole," S1N spat and was gone.

"Captain... if I may..." VAL said quietly, his smooth face the colour of milk.

"What is it?" Marrex muttered, settling himself into the battered captain's chair.

"S1N, for all his faults... well, I have to agree with him, sir."

Annoyed, Marrex turned to look at the AI. "What?"

VAL's face shrunk by half, but his eyes stayed the same size. "I think the boy is... *likeable*—even S1N is uncharacteristically taken with him. If... If Juniper is going to be with us for a while, until we figure out where to leave him, wouldn't it be nice to... I don't know... perhaps get to know him?"

"Why?"

Shrinking even further until he was no bigger than Marrex's thumb, VAL stared at him before replying. "You've been getting... *worse*. I worry about you, Captain."

Marrex grunted, looking away. "Leave me." He flicked one of the toggles on his chair arm, bringing up the field of stars on the big viewscreen. The AI was right—Marrex could feel himself withering away on the inside, day by day. The curse of his species. After a moment, he noticed VAL was still lingering within sight.

"Shall I ask S1N to have something made up for our young guest to eat?" the AI asked in a timid voice.

"Yes, fine," Marrex muttered.

"And, for yourself, sir?"

"I'm not hungry."

CHAPTER 3

THE STELLERION

Juniper paced the small room, back and forth from bed to closet, wondering what the hell he was going to do. Somewhere around his three hundredth circuit, his stomach gave a mighty squelch of hunger, and he groaned, trying to remember the last meal he'd eaten. Probably the greasy *taba* fries at the spaceport before he boarded the colony ship... seventeen years ago.

He turned back towards the bed and saw S1N curled up in a furry black ball on the blanket.

"*There* you are," Juniper said.

"Mmm?" The cat sounded half-asleep.

"I've been trying to reach you or VAL for a while."

"Mmmhm?"

S1N tucked his nose under his paw, and Juniper had to smile. He'd wanted a cat growing up. "Hey, can I ask why you look like that?"

One yellow-green eye opened, and then the other, followed by a jaw-cracking yawn. "Look like what?" S1N rolled over onto his side and extended all four feet in a stretch, fanning out his black jelly-bean toes. "What else would I look like?"

With a snort of amusement, Juniper shook his head at the cat. "You know, you're a funny sort of AI."

"Well, you're a funny sort of Human. What kind of a name is Juniper Bo anyway?" S1N didn't wait for his reply and just hopped down off the bed, the door to the room unlocking and sliding open as he got near it. "Come on... breakfast is served."

Juniper hesitated, looking at the dimly lit corridor beyond. "I'm not supposed to leave my quarters," he said quietly. His stomach gave another plaintive gurgle. "The captain said so."

"Pff. He's busy. Besides, what would you have me do? Wait on you in your room? Forget about it, Human." With tail up, S1N trotted quickly out of the room, and Juniper jumped to follow him before the door closed.

The corridor stretched in both directions, curving slightly, and was lit with cool recessed lights that brightened as Juniper passed them. The only noise he could hear besides his bare feet on the cold metal floor was a low mechanical rumble that he guessed was the ship's engines. After a few minutes, his stomach grumbled again, so he looked down at the cat padding along beside him, hoping to distract his hunger.

"So, what happened to me? Why was I on a shuttlecraft?" he asked. When he'd gone into stasis, it had been in a huge bay aboard the colony ship with eleven thousand other souls, each safe in their own pods.

"No clue," replied S1N, rising up into the air as if he were climbing invisible steps. "The shuttlecraft's computer was basically lobotomized in the accident. One sleeping Human and one missing Nelami pilot."

"Nelami? What would the Nelami want with *me*?" Juniper asked, confused. The Nelami were deep space scavengers and junk hawkers.

"Obviously, they thought they could make some money," S1N replied.

"But where did they find me? Why wasn't I aboard the colony ship to Rhesh-14?"

"Who knows?" S1N said dismissively. "Hey, why did you leave home anyway? Rhesh-14 is a real shithole. Were you on the run? Did you rob a bank? Renege on a deal?" The cat gave him a narrow, sidelong glance. "Seduce the wrong woman?"

Frowning, Juniper shook his head. "No, none of that. I left Terra Deux to make money."

"Oh?"

"My father is a merchant. Well, *was* a merchant. Massive solar flares wiped out pretty much his whole fleet, and we went from being rich to having to rely on charity in the span of two weeks. And on top of it all, my sisters had their betrothals annulled because Dad couldn't afford their dowries anymore."

"Bummer," S1N replied, floating along near Juniper's head.

Nodding, Juniper gave the cat a wry smile. "Yeah, that's one way of putting it."

"Your sisters couldn't pay their own way?"

"Not many jobs to be had back home, unfortunately. Not the kind my sisters would do."

"Whoring's too good for them, hm?" said the cat.

"That's not what I meant!" Juniper let out a bark of laughter. "Oh boy... Acacia and Willow, *prostitutes*? You don't know my sisters—they might be wearing second-hand clothes, but they're still *way* too precious in their own minds. They're selfish and spoiled rotten and used to having everything taken care of for them. Besides, I've got way more uh... experience than they do, but... my father would have had a heart attack if any of us had decided to earn money doing *that*."

"Does that experience include males?" S1N asked.

Wondering what was behind his question, Juniper side-eyed the AI and nodded. "Why? Is that a problem?"

"Why would it be a problem? I was just curious. You can do whatever you like with your meat-bag as far as I'm concerned."

Juniper snickered. "Well, I found a better way of making money with my 'meat-bag.' There was a hefty cheque that came with volunteering as a colonist. God, I wonder what happened to the ship..." Frowning, Juniper remembered then that it had been almost two decades since he'd left Terra Deux, and he felt a pang of worry. That money must have dried up long ago, and his family probably thought he was dead. "Do you think the captain would let me call home?"

"Maybe. But probably not."

Juniper frowned, wondering what the captain's problem was.

After a while, Juniper realized his legs were beginning to get sore. He didn't know if his hunger was messing with his sense of time, but it felt as if he'd been trudging down the corridor for at *least* ten minutes. "Hang on," he said, stopping. He leaned against the wall and squeezed his thigh.

The cat bounded ahead a few metres, then went down in a crouch, waiting for Juniper to catch up.

"How the hell big is this ship?" Juniper asked. The corridor had straightened out at some point while they were walking, and it just looked like an endless tunnel of doors and recessed lights.

"*Really* big," S1N replied, blinking slowly at him.

"Like, how much longer to the, um, place where we eat? What do you call it here?"

"Dining hall. We're almost there."

"All right, but how long is this corridor?"

"As long as it needs to be."

Juniper sighed, wishing it were the other AI accompanying him. At least VAL gave him halfway-straight answers.

"Fine. Let's just go."

MARREX BRUSHED some dark-red fur from the front of the black uniform and rolled his shoulders back, standing straighter. He glanced down again at his holocomm bracelet, staring at the coloured dots on the small screen. The Human was still in the dining hall.

Sighing, he adjusted his collar, then straightened the clasps on his cloak, wishing, for perhaps the first time since he'd come aboard, that he hadn't destroyed the big mirror in his quarters.

"Would you like me to show you how you look?" VAL asked as if reading his mind.

"No," Marrex growled. "Why?"

"Because judging by how you're fussing, I surmise you're thinking of going to the dining hall where Juniper is and you want to make a good impression."

"No," Marrex replied—but that was a lie, wasn't it?

"Then why do you keep looking to see where he is?"

Marrex's head snapped around, and he snarled at VAL who flew backwards in alarm. Embarrassed and furious, the captain ripped off the holocomm bracelet and threw it on the floor. Then he marched towards the bathroom and began unbuttoning his uniform. "I'm taking a bath, and when I'm out, I expect my breakfast to be waiting for me. And throw that out," he said, pointing to the bracelet on the floor.

"Yes, sir," VAL said, his face a very pale pink. "Very well, sir. I'll send a cleaning droid right away."

"And keep the Human away from me," Marrex growled, tearing off his undershirt. The follicles of his fur hurt from being pressed down for so long by his too-tight clothes. A bath would put him in better spirits. "Understand?"

"Yes, sir," VAL said quietly. "Understood."

CHAPTER 4
THE HIDDEN GARDEN

Burping, Juniper sat back in his chair and looked out the huge fibroglass viewport that made up the whole rear wall of the dining hall. He could see his pale translucent reflection on the window and only blackness and stars beyond—the same view that had greeted him at every mealtime in the twelve days since he'd been "thawed." With no departure to look forward to, and nothing productive to fill his days, Juniper was already bored with the routine he'd settled into to distract himself from his ambiguous status aboard the *Stellerion*.

Every morning, one of the AIs woke him for breakfast once the captain was on the bridge and the coast was clear. He'd take a quick particle shower, throw on a pair of shorts, and jog the entire kilometre and a half of hallway to the dining hall where he would eat the bizarre, sometimes disgusting dishes the replicators concocted for him. Then he would sit and digest while reading one of the trillion English-language books he had access to in the ship's entertainment database. The jog back to his room was followed by another shower, this time with water, then a nap or more reading. The afternoons he spent wandering the empty halls of the ancient Chato-class starship, aided by the holocomm bracelet VAL had found for him. It had a map of the ship with dots of colour showing where the entire crew was at that moment.

There were only four dots: green for Juniper, yellow for VAL, blue for S1N, and red for the captain.

Sighing, Juniper looked at the readout on the bracelet. S1N was curled up "asleep" or just ignoring him on the next table, and it looked like VAL was on the bridge. Almost two weeks and no one to talk to except two AIs whose base programs seemed to be corrupt, making it impossible to get any real information out of them. And he hadn't seen the captain since that first day.

Juniper glanced over at the tablet he'd been reading from over lunch. It was a book from Old Earth, back from before Contact. He was enjoying it—he really loved pre-Contact stuff —but he was extremely curious about something else and therefore antsy. For the last hour, the red dot on his bracelet had been motionless in a large unlabelled space on the map. It wasn't the captain's quarters—at night Juniper often watched the red dot moving restlessly on the other side of the ship where the captain slept—so what could the big room be, and why had the captain stayed there for so long? Juniper was dying to know.

The plan was simple enough. Juniper guessed he was being tracked around the ship by the bracelet he wore, so he was going to leave it in his room and head off by himself—he'd memorized the route easily enough.

He stood and started for the door, but immediately, there was a static crackle near his ear as S1N materialized like a weightless black parrot on his shoulder.

"Where are we going?"

"Um... I'm just going back to my room to take a nap."

"Oh," S1N replied, sounding disappointed, and Juniper wondered if the AIs got tired of being alone with each other so much—maybe he was a welcome distraction. The thought gave him a small pang of guilt for deceiving S1N, but he shrugged it off, laughing inwardly. He was so starved for interaction that he was projecting all sorts of things onto the ship's twin interfaces.

Faking a yawn, Juniper nodded. "Yeah, I'm bushed. That run this morning just wore me out."

S1N disappeared from his shoulder and reappeared in front of him, his yellow-green eyes wide and pupils down to mere slits. "The run didn't wear you down yesterday," the AI said a little suspiciously. "And you already took a nap today."

"Maybe my immune system is still acclimatising to the ship," Juniper tried. "I *am* feeling a little sluggish. Hey, you know what would help? If you could convince the replicators to make me some chicken noodle soup. God, I would love some chicken soup." The last bit wasn't a lie. Who knew he'd miss something so silly?

S1N let out a few mini-sneezes, whiskers trembling. "Chicken? Hmm... chicken... I'll see what I can do." And with that, the AI was gone.

Grinning, Juniper ran quickly back to his quarters, plumped some cushions under his bedcovers, and shoved the holocomm bracelet under the pillows. S1N's processes would be occupied with bullying the ancient replicators into twisting some protein strands into something resembling chicken noodle soup, and VAL was far too polite to bother him while he was taking a nap. He was free to explore on his own.

IT TOOK NEARLY HALF an hour to find the entrance to the mysterious room, but when he did, he just stood staring at the door nervously. There were symbols carved into it—not etched by laser but scored deep into the metal in brutal slashes, as though someone had written their message in a fury. Juniper reached out to touch one of them, curious, but the door slid open before he made contact. What lay beyond was nothing short of astonishing.

Eyes wide, Juniper stepped into a world of green and breathed in the humid, earthy air. The garden was beautiful and wild, nothing like he'd ever seen before. On Terra Deux, his family had had a small garden in a special greenhouse on their property—a few Earth ferns and rose bushes that had been genetically modified to withstand the perpetual drought and searing heat of the planet. After his father's entire fleet was destroyed by the monster solar flares, they could no longer afford the water for the garden, and the plants had turned to brown dust in less than a week.

Feeling overwhelmed by the lush foliage surrounding him, Juniper dashed away the tears that had welled up and laughed quietly to himself, his chest tight. Softly smiling, he decided to take the path to his left, stepping carefully on the smooth grey stones so he didn't damage the mossy ground cover. The path took him through a dense copse of trees that had big triangular leaves and pale stripes down their narrow trunks, then over a small wooden bridge with a babbling brook running beneath it. After the brook, he rounded a bend full of tall prickly shrubs and found himself surrounded by rose bushes of every imaginable colour. Nestled among the bushes and vines was a stone bench, and a little further away, as if guarding this sacred place, a marble statue of a creature that resembled a more graceful version of Captain Marrex. Looking up at the domed ceiling with its bright, warm lights, Juniper realized he had reached the centre of the hidden garden.

He cupped a pale-blue rose in his hand, careful to mind the thorns, and leaned in to smell it.

"What are you doing?" VAL said, appearing suddenly. "You can't be in here!"

Startled, Juniper took a step back. "I... I was..."

"If the captain catches you in here, he'll—" VAL stopped. "Are you *crying*?"

Wiping his tears away and feeling silly about shedding tears over trees and bushes, Juniper shrugged. "I was just walking around."

"Yes, well, you shouldn't be walking *here*. This is definitely and completely off-limits. *I'm* not even supposed to be here. Come now." The AI floated back along the path, then paused when he saw Juniper wasn't following. "You really must get out of here."

"What is this place?" Juniper asked, stalling. He didn't want to leave the rich, warm smell of living plants just yet. "I don't recognize some of these trees... are they from the captain's planet?"

"Yes. Well, most. Some of the roses are hybrids... Old Earth stock spliced with Ghelyx varietals."

"Ghelyx? Is that where the captain is from? I've never heard of it," Juniper lied as he ran his fingers along the curling leaf of what looked like a grapevine. He took another deep rose-scented breath, closing his eyes.

"Ghelyxians were part of the council that initiated Contact with Old Earth. Seeing as your species originated there, it surprises me that you didn't learn about them in school."

"Oh? I thought it was the Hoch who initiated Contact..." The light from above almost felt like real sunlight on Juniper's skin. Not the scorching twin suns of Terra Deux—no, this was like the life-giving Sol of Old Earth, a place he'd only read about.

"What sort of substandard education system did you have on Terra Deux? You should have learned about the—ohh, I see what you're doing. *Juniper Bo*," VAL said, sounding oddly like his sister Acacia when she was annoyed at him, "you're going to get us both in trouble if we don't get out of here *now*."

With a sigh, Juniper gazed back longingly at the little clearing with its bench and statue. It would be *just* the perfect place to sit and read in the afternoons, surrounded by flowers with only the lulling chatter of the stream in the background.

"Why is this off-limits?" he asked, pausing to pluck a small pink rose off a bush as he passed it. Seeing that it was thornless, he tucked it behind his ear, skipping over every second paving stone to keep up with VAL.

"It just is," VAL answered peevishly.

Juniper took one last look at the greenery and stepped out into the cold grey sterile hallway. He sighed. "How did you find me anyway?" he asked, starting back towards his quarters.

"I can track anything on the ship."

"Oh. It wasn't the bracelet then?"

"No." VAL's smooth face rippled from green to bright pink. "I want to commend you on how well you distracted S1N though. I'm afraid he might have to be rebooted."

"That bad, eh?" Juniper replied, worried he'd caused a mess of trouble, but VAL was smiling.

"He got himself into an infinite loop trying to force the replicators to comply to his request—every readout on the ship is showing the same word over and over."

"Chicken?" Juniper guessed with a laugh.

"That's it."

CHAPTER 5
JUNIPER SCREWS UP

"Captain?"

The captain lifted his head, startled, and turned towards the young man standing in the entrance to the dining hall.

Juniper's eyes widened and his face flushed. "I know I'm not supposed to be out of my quarters, but I wanted to apologize for disrupting the ship's navigation computer yesterday. I'm very sorry and I promise it won't happen again," he said in one breath.

Marrex stared at Juniper in silence for a few moments. The Human was wearing the top half of an Angorran deputy's uniform—an orange and red short-sleeved, high-collared jacket with glossy black buttons down the left side—and a pair of bright-green Melloran dance trousers. The pants were far too big for Juniper's slim build, but he'd cinched them tight at the waist with a yellow and orange silk scarf, its tasselled ends hanging down to his knee on one side. With his thick hair loose over his shoulders, the riotous colours of his clothes, and his feet bare, he looked like some kind of wild bohemian... but the effect was not unattractive.

"That's fine," Marrex muttered, looking back down at his

bowl of *rocklum* stew. Or at least that's what it was supposed to be... it tasted somewhat fishy. After a few seconds, he looked up again and saw Juniper had taken a few steps into the room and stood staring at him timidly. "What is it?"

"Can... I... um... join you?" asked Juniper. He had his hands jammed into his trouser pockets and elbows locked straight with shoulders held high.

Marrex was taken aback by both the request and Juniper's hope-filled expression.

"Who let you out of your room?" Marrex asked. "VAL?"

"Um, yeah. Don't be mad at him," Juniper said, taking another step towards Marrex. "I told VAL I wanted to apologize in person, and he agreed it was a good idea."

Marrex sighed. He had a feeling if he turned Juniper away, the AIs would conspire to throw the young man in his path again.

"Sit," he growled.

"Oh! Yes, sir," Juniper said, plunking down in the seat opposite the captain. "Thank you, sir."

Marrex nodded and let out a soft grunt, returning to his meal, but his hopes for a quiet supper were dashed when Juniper spoke up again.

"So, where are we going, anyway? S1N and VAL just say that our course avoids all planets and starports, but they won't tell me why. Is that why you can't drop me off somewhere? Are you on a secret mission?"

Frowning, Marrex spooned up another mouthful and chewed. After he'd swallowed with a grimace, he gave a headshake.

"Oh. Well, why won't they tell me where we're going? And for that matter, they're really tight-lipped about you too. I've tried asking them about you, you know, in case we ever talked I wanted to know a little about you so I didn't say something stupid... because I'm really grateful that you found me and everything..."

"Do you always talk so much?" Marrex asked, not looking up from his food.

Juniper let out an awkward laugh. "Um... only when I'm nervous. I've never met a Ghelyxian before. Or an Imperial captain, for that matter. I come from a pretty small town, and we don't really have many non-Humans and the only captains I've ever met were cargo ship captains..." Juniper trailed off as Marrex raised his head to stare at him. "Aaannd I'm talking again. I'll be quiet." He pressed his lips together and mimed locking them with a key and throwing it away.

Marrex snorted, then wiped his mouth with a napkin. Juniper just smiled at him in a friendly way. Finally, Marrex sighed again.

"They *can't* tell you anything about me except in a general sense. I won't allow it... their programming is locked."

Juniper's brows rose and he nodded silently.

"And it's not a secret mission. The *Stellerion* patrols the black for salvageable detritus."

Pointing to himself, Juniper cocked his head, and Marrex sat back, crossing his arms.

"This is becoming tedious. Talk."

"Thank you." Juniper grinned wide. "You mean like the shuttlecraft you found me in?"

"Yes, exactly."

"Did you piss someone off?" Juniper asked.

"What?" Marrex sat up straighter, fixing Juniper with a hard stare.

"You know, to get such a terrible, lonely posting. Or... did you request it?"

Marrex snorted again, not knowing what to think of this conversation. He wasn't used to talking, much less talking about himself, and Juniper seemed primed to delve into his business. However, for some reason it wasn't really bothering him that much. Maybe it was because Juniper seemed honestly interested in engaging him... maybe it was because he was such a treat on the eyes and smelled as good as he looked. Whatever it was, Marrex felt himself mellowing in the young man's presence and it was... nice.

"You're not afraid of me," he said, ignoring Juniper's questions.

Juniper looked confused, narrowing his dark eyes at the captain. "Why would I be afraid of you?"

From Marrex's experience, many smaller humanoids found even healthy Ghelyxians a touch intimidating. With his extensive deformities, Marrex was surprised that Juniper had no problems looking at him.

"Are you planning on doing something... um, unpleasant to me?" Juniper said. "Because you don't seem like that kind of guy to me. Yeah, maybe you're a bit standoffish, but I don't believe that someone who takes the time to maintain such a beautiful garden could be the kind of—"

Alarmed, Marrex growled, leaning forward so his face was close to Juniper's. "Who told you about the garden?"

"Oh. Ha ha. Well, I-I found it yesterday, and it really is very, *very* lovely..." Juniper's breaths came in small huffs and the fear was plain in his eyes, but he held Marrex's gaze and didn't back away.

Flaring his nostrils, Marrex bared his fangs, furious that his sacred space had been violated.

"VAL!" Marrex roared, and the AI appeared immediately, pale and transparent.

"Yes... Captain?" VAL whispered nervously.

"Take him back to his room, and he's not to come out again until I say so. No exceptions."

Juniper's face had gone ashen. "I'm sorry, Captain. I am so sorry."

Marrex watched VAL escort Juniper out of the dining hall. As soon as they were out of sight, he stood and brought down both fists hard on the table, denting the metal and sending his bowl flying.

"I MESSED UP. Fuck, I messed up really bad," Juniper kept repeating as he followed VAL down the corridor.

"It's not... *that* bad," VAL said, but his tone was unconvincing.

"I'm so stupid," Juniper groaned. "Why did I mention the garden?"

"Because you're a big fucking idiot," S1N answered, jumping out of thin air to begin walking upside down on the ceiling.

Grimacing, Juniper just nodded. "I am. I really am."

"And you're not forgiven for jamming up my system," the cat added.

"I didn't know it was going to cause so much trouble..." Juniper felt so low he thought he was going to start crying.

"I was trying to do something *nice* for you, and I almost never go out of my way to do anything nice for anyone," S1N replied primly.

"It's true," VAL agreed. "He doesn't."

"I am so sorry," Juniper said, rubbing his face. "God, I wish I could just take back the last two days." But that wasn't really true—he would have missed the lush greenery of the wonderful hidden garden, and he wouldn't change that experience for a million credits. However, now that he knew the garden was there, it was always in his thoughts. No wonder he had mentioned it to the captain. Remembering what had prompted him to bring it up, he said, "He and I were having a perfectly pleasant conversation, and then he suddenly asked me why I wasn't afraid of him. I know you two aren't able to answer questions about him in any kind of detail... but can you give me a clue about why he thought I would be afraid? Has he hurt people? Is this why he's basically in exile?"

"How do you know he's exiled?" VAL asked, his face going bright yellow.

"I figure no one would take such a lonely, depressing post unless they were trying to get away from everyone *or* if they were forced to take it because of something they'd done."

S1N and VAL exchanged a glance and then both fixed on Juniper.

"Have you ever seen a Ghelyxian before?" asked S1N. The tip of his tail twitched, and the cat did a slow barrel roll in the air until he was hovering in front of Juniper's face.

"No. Never. Why?"

"Do you know what they're supposed to look like?"

"Um... not really. Should I?"

"You weren't kidding about the lousy school system on Terra Deux, were you?" VAL said.

Juniper let out a short laugh and shrugged. "Yeah, it was pretty basic. The solar flares that hit Terra Deux all the time fry electronics and knock out power grids. Big cities like Gatineau and Marseille have good shielding so their libraries are pretty complete, but in Port-Cartier where I lived, we didn't have much. Not a single up-to-date database. You ever seen a chalkboard?"

"Erm, no?" VAL replied.

"Well, I have," Juniper said with a wry grin. He wondered whether his father and sisters still lived in Port-Cartier. Maybe he'd find out one day if he hadn't completely wrecked his chances of calling home. "The only reason we were out in the boonies was because Dad liked having a big house. Can't have that in a city... But, in the end, right before I left, the house was almost empty. My dad sold most of the furniture—and some of it had been in the family for *generations*—just to keep the lights on." Juniper shook himself out of his memories, aware that the two AIs were soberly watching him as they kept pace. Even S1N looked concerned.

"I'm sorry. What were you saying about Ghelyxians?" Juniper asked, feeling tired and lonely on top of the disappointment he felt over his gaffe with Captain Marrex.

"I can't get into specifics about the captain, and he's purged some records from the system... but Ghelyxian *biology* might interest you," S1N said in a quiet voice.

"Does it have to do with the captain thinking I should be afraid of him?" Juniper said, curious about what they were driving at.

"Yes," VAL said, sounding inspired. "Shall I pull up those sections of the database in your quarters?"

"Sure. Why not. I've got all the time in the world now, don't I?" Juniper replied with a sigh.

THE SUN SHONE on Juniper's face, and he smiled, stretching out on the soft grass with his hands behind his head. Two purple butterflies twirled and fluttered overhead, and the breeze was warm and smelled of flowers. Juniper couldn't remember the last time he'd been so happy and comfortable. Not for a long time.

When a shadow crept slowly across his chest, Juniper sat up, shading his eyes. It came from the small statue of the Ghelyxian he'd seen in the captain's garden. As if his noticing it brought it to life, the statue stepped down from its pedestal and hopped towards Juniper. Slowly, the stone changed colour, its pelt becoming a glossy red and its two horns—not four— turning black. Instead of sharp yellow fangs, it had a mouth of somewhat blunter white teeth, and the claws at the ends of its small hands were short and not hooked like the captain's. Now that Juniper knew *this* was what a healthy Ghelyxian was supposed to look like, thanks to the ship's database, he felt he understood the captain's surly demeanor a little better.

The miniature Ghelyxian peered curiously at Juniper, tilting its head to get a better look at him, and Juniper noticed that it was completely naked—and not only that... it was sporting a rather proud erection.

Funny how that always happens in dreams, thought Juniper. *One minute you're doing something normal—the next, someone naked comes along.* He definitely knew it was a dream, there was no other way he could be lying where he was, being scrutinized by a naked Ghelyxian manikin.

"I wonder... do you like me?" he asked and let out a slow breath when he saw he was naked too. *Funny dreams.*

The small Ghelyxian nodded and pointed to Juniper.

"What is it?" he asked, getting onto his hands and knees. "Do you want to know if I like you too?"

The creature nodded again, then pointed down to its cock. It was red like its pelt all the way to the base of the narrow head where it was ringed twice in black. At the tip of it, there was a black pattern like butterfly's wings around the double slit.

"I *do* like you," Juniper said, finding himself getting aroused by the sight of the Ghelyxian's cock.

He'd gone to bed right after scouring the database for information on the captain's species, and obviously, the sexual anatomy diagrams were fresh in his mind. He just wished they'd been properly labelled. Why the second meatus? What was it for?

"Hey, are you supposed to represent the captain? Wait—"

The little Ghelyxian ran a few steps in the other direction, then looked back at Juniper, gesturing him to follow. Juniper got to his feet and found that he was not much bigger than the statue-come-to-life. Together they pushed through the thick bushes, leaves like hands stroking the length of Juniper's body, making him shiver.

"Where are we going?" he asked, panting. "Can we stop? I want to... Hey, wait!"

The creature disappeared into the thicket, and Juniper lost sight of it. When he emerged into the clearing, he saw that the statue had returned to its pedestal, but this time it had four twisted horns, and its fangs were bared. The garden around the statue of Captain Marrex had gone brittle and brown. A terrible sadness hung in the air, silent and oppressive.

"I want to help you!" Juniper shouted. He could feel tears rolling down his cheeks, his arousal forgotten. There was just so much *pain* in the captain's face, so much self-loathing. "What do I do?"

The statue of Captain Marrex wobbled on its pedestal and then tipped over. Before Juniper could catch it, it fell to the ground where it shattered into a thousand pieces, black blood oozing from every shard.

JUNIPER OPENED HIS EYES, the strange dream already fading. He was alone in his narrow bed, the room empty, but he had the strangest impression that someone had been standing over him while he slept. Feeling unsettled, he pulled the blanket higher on his shoulder and frowned. Something seemed... different about his room. It took a few minutes before he noticed the rose he had taken from the garden was gone.

CHAPTER 6
THE ACCIDENT

"You don't understand," Juniper groaned, clutching at his head. "I am *literally* going crazy. I have to get out. Please? Please, just let me out into the hallway? I'll do *anything*."

"I'm afraid I can't do that, Juniper," VAL said, his projected face a sickly shade of puce. "I can't go against the captain."

"I can't stand another minute of this. I've been locked in this room for a week!" They'd even taken away his holocomm bracelet.

"Pff. A week is nothing," S1N said, lying on his back on the bed with all four paws in the air. "Do you want to rewatch that movie about the dog and the cat finding their way home? I liked that one."

"No!" Juniper closed his eyes and took a few deep breaths. "I want to get out and stretch my legs. See something other than these four walls. I need to get out. *Please*. I'm claustrophobic."

"You spent seventeen years in a box the size of a coffin," the cat pointed out.

"I was *asleep*," he replied through clenched teeth. When he looked up, the two AIs were just staring at him mutely.

After a moment, VAL said, "Well, we *could* give you something to sleep..." But he fell silent under Juniper's withering glare.

Setting his jaw, Juniper marched resolutely to the door and skimmed his hands along the walls to each side of it, looking for a crack or a hidden panel.

"What are you doing?" VAL asked.

"If you're not going to let me out, then I'm going to find a way out myself," Juniper replied, finding a seam. He tried to pry it open with his nails but couldn't get it to budge. With a sigh, he kept looking and, after a few more fruitless passes with his fingers, decided to investigate the door itself. It was the kind that slid from one side to the other when it opened, but Juniper could see the edge if he pressed his cheek against the metal. An idea came to him.

Juniper went and grabbed the knife from his plate, and he jammed it into the side of the door, trying to wedge the knife under the edge so he'd get leverage enough to pry the door open.

"You really shouldn't do that," S1N said, sounding concerned. "You might screw up the door so it won't open at all... and then what does that accomplish?"

"I don't know. I just need to get ou—*fuck*!" Juniper dropped the knife and clutched his hand, gasping as blood welled up from a deep cut at the base of his thumb. The old fibroplastic had cracked through with his efforts, and the tang, though duller than the blade, had nearly gone through his hand. "Oh god. Holy shit." He stumbled back to his lunch tray and grabbed the napkin, wrapping it around his hand. Almost immediately, blood began seeping through the fabric.

"Well, that's no good," S1N said, sitting up. He stared at Juniper's hand, his tail twitching.

"Are you all right?" VAL asked, hovering closer.

"Does it look like I'm all right?" Juniper said hoarsely. He'd never been good at the sight of blood, and this was a *lot* of blood. He felt nauseous and faint. "Let me out. I have to get to the med bay. Where is it?"

For a few seconds, neither AI responded.

"Ah... We can't do that," VAL finally said. "Captain's orders."

"What?" Juniper teetered where he stood and decided to sit on the floor before he fell over. "Screw the captain and screw his orders. Can't you see I'm going to bleed to death?"

"Well. Uh. Hm" was all VAL said.

"I need... medical attention," Juniper whispered, his heart pounding and mouth dry. "You *have* to help me." Blood was running down his arm and dripped on his pants. He put his head back against the side of the bed, fear making his vision murky. *"Please."*

Juniper realized there was no one to help him. He was on a ship with no crew. The AIs were only holoprojections. They could control the ancient service droids strewn around the ship to deliver his food and do simple things that didn't require much dexterity, but while they could get one of them to bring a suture gun to the room, Juniper would bleed to death in the meantime. He let out a rasping sob, then tried to calm himself, preparing to stand. There had to be something in his room that would work as a tourniquet.

However, as soon as he got to his feet, Juniper saw the floor rushing up to meet his face...

MARREX SQUATTED DOWN on his haunches, peering at the unconscious young man on the floor. Then he glared up at the two AIs hovering close.

"You two are morons," he said.

"You said no exceptions, Captain," VAL replied defensively. "I was only following orders."

"Yeah, that's not fair," S1N said, slinking closer. "You can't just give 'no exception' orders willy-nilly and expect us to—"

"Go," Marrex growled, tucking his arms under Juniper's prone body and lifting him up gently.

"I should get credit for calling you," added the cat, but he winked out before Marrex could say anything.

With a sigh, Marrex set the young man down on the bed and shook his head.

JUNIPER SLOWLY OPENED HIS EYES, feeling weird and heavy. The lights were low, and he was lying in his bed, snug under the covers. For a few seconds, he lay there quietly, thinking about the dream he'd just had. Another one about the garden and the statue. The dream came almost every night now, though always with small changes—this time it had been night in the garden, with fireflies zinging around as he chased the statue back to its pedestal. The air had felt heavy with rain, something he'd never experienced in real life. There had been a sense of urgency... Juniper frowned, trying to remember the rest, but couldn't.

Lifting his hand to his face to rub sleep from his eyes, he froze—there was something white wrapped around it. Suddenly, the memory of his injury came back to him, and he stared at the neat bandage in wonder. Who had patched him up?

He sat up, a bit dizzy, and touched his head. Wincing, he found a tender lump where his head had met with the floor. It was sore but bearable.

In a daze, Juniper slid out of bed. He was shirtless but wearing a strange pair of thin, calf-length blue pants that fit him like a glove. Another mystery. Who had dressed him?

Then he saw the door to his room was wide open.

"VAL?" he called. "S1N?" When no one appeared, he took a few steps, cradling his arm against his chest, and peered out into the corridor. "Hello?"

Nervous but intrigued, he walked along the corridor, calling to the AIs every few minutes, but when all he was met with was more silence, he began to lose his nerve. Juniper paused, wondering if he should just go back to his room when he noticed twinkling lights at the far end of the corridor. He straightened his shoulders, trying not to let his nerves get the best of him, and continued until he had reached a big open door. At the far end of the dark room, there were stars, a whole field of them, clearer and brighter than what could be seen from any other viewport on the ship. In awe, he stepped into the room, wanting to get a better look.

"You're awake," said a gruff voice to the left of him.

Slowly, the lights brightened until he could see the big chair at the centre of the room, the captain slouching comfortably in it with one booted foot up on the railing in front of him.

Juniper opened his mouth to speak but had to clear his throat. "I am," he replied quietly. Looking down at his bandaged hand, he wrinkled his brow. "Is... is it you I have to thank for saving me?"

Captain Marrex snorted but didn't turn to look at him. He still gazed at the stars up on the big viewscreen, and Juniper studied his profile. He could see where the captain's deformities had pushed forward his bottom jaw and blurred the edges between the Ghelyxian's already short nose and wide mouth, creating the illusion of a crude snout. He wondered what the captain had looked like when he was young.

"Was that... a laugh?" he asked cautiously.

This time Captain Marrex looked over at him, his expression impossible to read.

"I don't think I 'saved' you."

"I was bleeding to death."

Captain Marrex snorted again, and the amusement in it was unmistakable this time. "Unlikely. It was a minor cut."

"It was? There was so much blood."

"It had already stopped by the time I arrived."

"Oh," Juniper replied, feeling sheepish.

"You were out cold for an unusually long time... You're a bit delicate, aren't you?"

"I've never been good at bleeding," Juniper admitted. He touched the bump on his head again. Smiling, he shrugged. "Or falling, I guess."

Captain Marrex stared at him in silence, and Juniper's smile faded.

"Ah... er... How did you know I was hurt?"

"You have S1N to thank for that."

"Oh?" Juniper crossed his arms over his chest, feeling a bit exposed under the captain's unblinking gaze. "Where is he, anyway? And VAL... I tried calling them."

"They're busy running system checks as punishment for taking my orders so literally."

"Ah." Juniper pushed a hank of hair out of his face. "Um. Well, thank you for helping me. I really appreciated it."

The captain turned back to the star field, the chair creaking loudly as he shifted. "Go now."

Startled by the abrupt dismissal, Juniper took a few steps towards the open door, then paused. "Captain?"

Captain Marrex grunted.

"Am I to stay locked in my room again?" he asked in a low voice.

"No. Just don't wander where you're not supposed to. Understood?"

"Yes, sir. Thank you! I promise..." Juniper remembered how the captain had reacted to his babbling before and stopped.

Without another word, he left the brooding captain behind on the bridge, his heart light. Juniper was still a virtual prisoner, but he was confident that it was only temporary.

He would win the captain's trust... and he had an idea of where to start.

CHAPTER 7
MAKING CHANGES

S1N watched the captain lift the spoon to his mouth. If he'd had any lungs or any need to breathe, the AI would have been holding his breath. Only his tail twitched, an unfortunate affectation that was part of his programming he couldn't control, as he waited anxiously for Marrex to take his first taste.

Captain Marrex's brow creased as the broth touched his tongue, and after he swallowed, he frowned into the bowl. Slowly, he lifted his head and fixed S1N with a wide-eyed stare.

"What is this?"

"*Delpi* soup. What you asked for," S1N replied, terse from apprehension.

The captain took another spoonful of the traditional Ghelyxian autumn soup and shook his head slowly.

"What is it? Does it taste bad?" asked the AI.

"No."

The captain's voice was quiet with amazement, and S1N had to stop himself from leaping around like a fool from relief. Scanning the captain, S1N saw that his pleasure hormones were elevated and his pulse had quickened. The AI had been skeptical about Juniper's plan, but it seemed he knew what he was doing.

"How?" Marrex demanded in his typical laconic way, and took another slow sip, swallowing it with obvious enjoyment.

"Juniper."

Again, the captain's brow creased up with astonishment.

"Juniper did this?"

"Yes," replied S1N a little smugly.

"Go get him. Now."

"Yes, sir!"

HANDS CLASPED BEHIND HIM, Juniper walked into the dining hall, trying to project more confidence than he was feeling, all the while worrying he'd overshoot it and wind up in the realm of cocky... which he was sure the captain wouldn't appreciate. So, he lowered his gaze as he approached the table where Captain Marrex was seated and let out a silent, slow breath to calm himself.

"You called for me, Captain?" he murmured respectfully.

"You fixed the replicators?"

Juniper slowly lifted his head and offered only a nod.

"Who told you to do that?" asked Captain Marrex.

For a second, Juniper was at a loss. Had he screwed up again? It was impossible to tell whether the captain was pleased or not.

"I... I took the initiative," he replied. "I'm sorry if I—"

"Good work."

Juniper blinked rapidly a few times, then looked down and noticed that there were three bowls in front of the captain, all of them scraped clean.

"Thank you, sir," he said in a rush, and smiled wide.

"How did you do it?"

"The protein filters were completely clogged, and I noticed there was a small hole between the reclamation port and the extractor so... well, things were getting mixed up and the replicator was compensating but not able to filter," he explained as concisely as he could.

The captain nodded his horned head but didn't speak.

"And... I can do other things," Juniper ventured.

"What things?"

"Well, the other day, I noticed your captain's chair—"

"What's wrong with my chair?" Captain Marrex asked abruptly, sitting up.

"It's... tilted to the side. And it looks like the bolts holding it are about to give any second."

"And you can fix that?" A wrinkle appeared in the middle of the captain's forehead where the fur was very short.

"I can. See, I figured out what's wrong with your ship—uh, not that there's anything *wrong* with it," Juniper added quickly. "But you're short-handed... *Literally* short of hands."

"Hm."

"I know you've been doing most of the repairs yourself, but there's a limit to what one man can take on." Juniper wasn't sure, but he thought he saw the captain's nostrils flare a bit and his eyes widen at his use of the word *man*. "It's all fine and good to rely on VAL and S1N to handle the ship's systems, but you need an actual pair of hands to take care of physical repairs to the ship." He held his hands up, the right one still bandaged, and smiled. "And, repairs to you and me."

To his surprise, Captain Marrex let out what sounded like an honest-to-goodness laugh, and Juniper grinned wider.

"All right. Fix my chair," the captain said. Then he frowned at Juniper as if only just noticing something. "Why are you wearing that?"

Juniper glanced down at the ugly dull-grey jumpsuit he'd found in a utility closet that morning.

"I don't know. I thought maybe you'd prefer me looking more... professional?"

Snorting, Captain Marrex tossed his head as he stood up. "Wear whatever you want."

"You don't have a preference?" Juniper asked. The jumpsuit was uncomfortable compared to the mismatched outfits he'd managed to put together from the clothing he'd scavenged all over the ship.

"No." The captain stared down at him, his black, pupilless eyes narrowed.

Juniper waited, sensing the captain wasn't finished with him.

"Actually, yes," Captain Marrex said gruffly as he turned to go. "I liked how you were dressed before." Without another word, the captain left the dining hall.

"Wow," said S1N, appearing next to Juniper.

"What?" Juniper asked, his cheeks warm and stomach full of silly butterflies flitting about.

"That went well," S1N replied, blinking his eyes slowly at Juniper in contentment.

"It did, didn't it?" Juniper leaned over to press the button on the table and watched the dishes slide into the refabricator. Then he looked back up at the door through which the captain had departed, and smiled.

MARREX PULLED up the ship's schematic on the reclaimed holocomm bracelet. Again. The green dot representing Juniper was still in the observation deck. *What is he doing?* It was late—usually the Human had settled in by now. Frowning, Marrex rubbed his face, wishing he could stop thinking about the young man. Juniper kept extending what seemed like a hand of friendship, but that had to be a ruse... didn't it? He growled

48

under his breath and turned off the bracelet's screen, lying back against the pillows. Marrex could easily drop the Human off at any planet or station beyond Imperial space and let him find his own way home. He *should*. But... he couldn't bring himself to do it. Outside Imperial law, beautiful Juniper would be snatched up by the first xeno flesh-peddler who laid eyes on him. Or would he? Maybe he could take care of himself.

Maybe there's another reason you're keeping him here.

Marrex stared at the green dot, realizing he'd turned the screen back on again without thinking.

"Good god... Why don't you just go see what he's doing?"

Marrex snorted and turned to S1N, who was sitting primly on the small shelf next to the bed.

"What concern is it of yours?"

"Sir?"

Snorting again, Marrex shook his head. "Don't 'sir' me. What is it?"

S1N licked his paw and passed it over his ear, before answering. "Well... you were... happy earlier. About the soup." His ear twitched, and he gave it another swipe with his paw. "I've never seen you happy."

"Why do you care if I'm happy?"

"I just thought you might enjoy a change from your relentless brooding," S1N replied with a swish of his tail. "I don't really care. Do what you want."

THE OBSERVATION DECK was dark and silent, lit only by the stars beyond the viewport, and for a moment, Marrex thought he might have missed Juniper. However, his eyes picked out subtle movement on one of the large comfortable lounge chairs, and he took a quiet step into the room to get a better look.

The Human was sitting with his knees up to his chest, arms wrapped around them, his head tilted back as he watched the glittering beauty of the aBi nebula. How different he was than the two Humans Marrex had encountered before... They'd been oily and unshaven and brutish, but maybe that was because they were underworld darkmarket junk hawkers. Maybe Juniper was what Humans were *supposed* to look like.

No. Marrex gave a little headshake. He had a feeling Juniper was unique. But what *was* it that so appealed to him? Was it the long flawless limbs? The interesting lines of his smooth muscles, so different from his own? The way the light played with the gold in his eyes? Or was it the long dark hair that called to Marrex? He could imagine himself running his hands through it, burying his face in Juniper's neck...

"I never knew anything could be so beautiful," Juniper said in a hushed voice.

Marrex's heart stopped in his chest, and it took him a few breathless seconds to realize Juniper was talking about the stars.

Marrex stared at Juniper's starlit profile. "Yes... beautiful," he said, his throat dry.

Juniper slowly turned to the captain, his expression lost to the dark.

Marrex turned his face away, uncomfortably aware of Juniper's gaze. "I'm sorry, I didn't mean to disturb you."

"That's all right. I was about to go to bed." Juniper rose gracefully out of his seat. "Will you walk with me, Captain?"

Marrex couldn't think of anything to say, so he just gave a brusque nod and gestured for Juniper to lead the way out of the observation deck.

Side by side, they walked silently down the corridor. Marrex kept glancing at Juniper out of the corner of his eye, wondering what was going on inside the young man's mind to make him so quiet. The corridor was a bit narrow for the both of them, and as they walked, their arms occasionally brushed, sending Marrex's fur ruffling up his back—a ticklish, exciting feeling. He clenched his jaw, wishing he had something interesting to say to distract himself from the closeness of the Human, but too soon Juniper stopped in front of a metal door.

"Well, this is me," Juniper said, looking up at Marrex with a smile.

"Ah... yes."

"I'll come see you tomorrow after breakfast."

"Tomorrow?"

"For your chair."

"Right." Marrex frowned, then nodded. "All right."

"Goodnight, Captain."

"Goodnight... Juniper."

The Human pressed the button, and the door slid open with a hiss. Juniper walked into his room and shot another smile over his shoulder at Marrex before the door closed.

Marrex panted a few breaths, the fur on his back standing on end again, and closed his eyes. Then he let out a sigh and started off towards his own room.

What could he trust—his instincts or common sense? For the first time in his life, they were completely at odds with each other.

CHAPTER 8
DINNER, DINNER?

Captain Marrex watched Juniper reattach the panel on the chair arm, the tip of the Human's tongue sliding out of the corner of his mouth as he concentrated on reconnecting wires. He was wearing the bright-green Melloran dance trousers again, but this time, they were paired with a sleeveless mesh top in dark pink... another odd combination. Not that he was complaining—he could see Juniper's skin through the mesh, and it was tantalizing to catch glimpses of the two dimples in his lower back. Occasionally, when Juniper bent lower, Marrex saw the full triangle of his sacrum pointing to a tiny hint of his cleft above the waist of his pants. He let out a slow sigh, feeling a bit ashamed of himself for staring, but it was hard not to. When Juniper turned around, Marrex's gaze followed the smooth line of his groin.

"Captain?"

Marrex lifted his eyes, startled. "Yes? What is it?" he asked, feeling like a youngling caught with his hand in the *sheppik* jar.

"I said, why don't you sit and try it out?"

Was Marrex imagining it, or did Juniper look flushed? He just nodded and went to his chair, sinking down into it. It felt odd at first—he'd gotten so used to its rightward tilt, but it didn't squeak when he moved, nor did it shimmy like it normally did when he sat back. He flicked the toggle switch for the viewscreen, and it came on.

"Now try the others," Juniper said, standing next to the chair.

Curious, Marrex flipped the next switch, and the view changed to infrared, revealing to the naked eye the hidden stars of the aBi nebula. "Huh," he said, flipping it back and forward again. "I'd almost forgotten it did that." One by one, he tried the toggles, rediscovering functions he'd thought long lost.

After a moment, he realized Juniper was gazing at him with a strange expression on his face.

"What?" Marrex felt self-conscious. Not many people could bear to look at him that long, but Juniper seemed to have no problem with it.

"How long have you been alone on this ship?" Juniper asked.

Marrex gave a short bitter laugh. Instead of answering, he called out, "S1N?"

From atop the unused science station came S1N's sleepy voice. "Sixty-three point four five years, Imperial Standard," the AI said.

Marrex heard Juniper's swift intake of breath, and he turned to the young man, wryly amused by his reaction.

"That's—" Juniper's forehead wrinkled as he did the math. "About a hundred and twelve years back home." Shaking his head, the young man looked at him in awe. "No wonder you're such a..."

"Such a *what*?" Marrex said it with a warning growl, but he was surprised to realize he was only teasing.

"Such a good *captain*," Juniper finished with a bright grin, but he laughed a little nervously.

Marrex chuckled, sitting back in his repaired chair and gazed at his new guest-cum-crewmate. Juniper had put his thick dark hair up into a pile on top of his head, and it should have looked ridiculous... but it didn't. It showed off the strong line of his jaw, the graceful length of his neck, and his perfect delicate ears. Juniper's smile went shy under the captain's scrutiny, and Marrex thought about the subtle tension between them the night before... Had he only imagined it?

"Your face is dirty," Marrex said gruffly. Juniper had a dark streak of oil across his forehead. "Go clean up. Come to the dining hall when you're done."

"Why?" Juniper tucked his pliers into the pocket of his trousers, searching the captain's expression. "Is there something to fix?"

"No. I would like to have dinner with you."

Juniper inspected himself in the mirror. His face was clean, and he'd taken his hair down and given it a good brushing—it fell, shiny and dark past his shoulders, with a few chin-length pieces framing his face. Smiling at his reflection, he thought he looked pretty good.

"What in the world are you wearing?" S1N asked from the bed.

"It used to be a funny sort of dress. I *think* it might have belonged to the wife of the Angorran who was stationed on the *Stellerion* before the captain took command. Pieces of it were rotted away—I'm guessing natural fibers of some kind—but I sewed the bottom together to make pants... sort of." He looked down at the short blue-and-yellow-patterned pants and tugged them down a bit. It was a good thing that Angorran women weren't curvy like Human women. The bodice was tight and lay flat across his ribs, and the arms were short, but he figured that matched the bottom half.

"You can sew?" The cat sounded vaguely impressed.

55

"I watched a whole lot of instruction vids," replied Juniper, belting his creation with a length of shiny orange fabric. "I figure I did ok."

"Well, I think he looks very nice," VAL said.

"Did I say he *didn't* look nice?" S1N said, leaping off the bed, his tail a sinuous black *S* behind him. He stopped by Juniper's feet, looking up at him round-eyed. "You look very nice, Juniper."

"Thanks, you two. I don't even know what to expect. Did he ask me for *dinner* dinner or is this just...? I don't know." Juniper sighed, turning his makeshift belt so the knot was over his hip.

"You'll do *just* fine," VAL replied, the AI's smooth face a pretty shade of periwinkle.

"Well, as long as you don't keep him waiting. I don't know if you noticed, but he's a little short on patience," S1N said, his whiskers twitching.

"Right," Juniper said, squaring his shoulders. "Let's go."

MARREX FROWNED at the tablet in his hand, reading over the paragraph he'd just read for the third time. It wasn't that the book wasn't good, quite the opposite, but he was suffering a lapse in attention because every little sound caused him to look up at the door with nervous anticipation. He sighed, shaking his head, and tried to concentrate on the prose.

It was an ancient novel written on pre-Contact Earth about an English governess and her employer. It was a lively, interesting narration, very different from what he was used to, and though he'd had to translate some of the obsolete words, he had—when he could rally his attention—been rather enjoying it. Another sound caused him to lift his head, and this time, instead of the random clicks and hums of the old ship, it was Juniper standing at the door to the dining hall.

Marrex could not keep himself from staring. The young man was wearing a curious ensemble of yellow and blue, belted with an orange sash, but the bodice, if that's what it was, stopped just below Juniper's bare nipples. It was... stunning.

"Can I come in?" asked the young man in his velvety smooth voice, and Marrex nodded quickly, rising to his feet.

Finding his voice, the captain said, "You look"—then he stumbled. Beautiful? Handsome? Pretty? What was the appropriate word?—"nice," he finished lamely.

Juniper smiled at him. "Thank you."

"Sit. Please."

Marrex noticed the two AIs hanging back. S1N's tail was lashing and VAL looked nervous—the captain frowned at them. "Go. Don't return unless called."

"Yes, sir," they said in unison, and Marrex's brow wrinkled up. He'd expected more resistance.

Reclaiming his seat across from Juniper, Marrex sat back, wishing he'd rehearsed some topic of conversation. "Thank you for fixing my chair."

"Don't mention it. I'm pretty good with my hands. When my dad lost his fortune, we couldn't afford to keep the staff at the house anymore. I ended up doing almost everything myself... fixing the relays on the roof, re-surfacing the launch port, changing the intake filters... that kind of thing."

Marrex nodded.

"So, what are we eating? Are the replicators still up to snuff?"

Nodding again, Marrex keyed in the meal he'd planned and watched them materialize on the table.

"What is it?" Juniper asked, looking curiously at all the small metal dishes. "Do we share everything?"

"Yes. It's known simply as a 'sharing meal' where I'm from. It's not very sophisticated—I hope you don't mind. I wasn't sure what your tastes are, and this is a bit of everything that is compatible with your digestive system. If you'd like, I can replicate something..." he trailed off when he saw Juniper staring at him with a wide smile. Marrex snorted and tossed his head. "If you're so *amused* by my choices, *you* pick," he growled defensively.

Juniper lifted a hand in alarm, shaking his head quickly. "No! No, it's not that. This looks wonderful, thank you, Captain. Don't be so touchy—I was just smiling because I like hearing you speak... you're usually rather, ah... concise."

"Oh." Marrex frowned. "I..." He sighed, not knowing what to say.

"You've been alone for a long time, Captain. I get it. It's ok," Juniper replied. "But I do like it when you talk for more than two or three words at a time. You have a wonderful accent."

"I... do?"

"*I* think so," Juniper said with a nod. He grinned at Marrex's stupefaction, then pointed to the dishes. "Now tell me what everything is and how I'm supposed to eat it."

Marrex nodded again, cleared his throat, and started describing each dish... trying not to be self-conscious about his accent while also forcing himself to accept Juniper's exclamations for what they were: honest enthusiasm.

JUNIPER TOOK another sip from his glass. The cold drink was creamy and tasted like almonds and cinnamon, but was also a little salty and maybe a bit fizzy. He decided that it was the most delicious thing he'd ever had before.

"What is this called again?" he asked.

"*Leb.* And don't drink too much of it, or else you won't sleep a wink tonight," said Captain Marrex.

"Oh. Ok," Juniper said, setting down the glass. He smiled at the captain.

They hadn't said more than a dozen words during the multidish meal, but he could see the Ghelyxian had genuinely started to relax in his presence. The captain had rolled up the sleeves of the white dress shirt he wore and undone the top button, and he was lounging back in his chair comfortably, picking at the last of his meal.

"Thank you. That was delicious," Juniper said.

Captain Marrex bobbed his head in a bow and let out a small pleased-sounding grunt.

Wishing he could pull the captain into a real conversation, Juniper looked at the tablet resting near the Ghelyxian's elbow.

"You were reading something when I came in earlier. Can I ask what it was?"

The lines deepened in Captain Marrex's brow, and Juniper worried he was being too nosy. He was surprised when the captain just slid the tablet across to him. Juniper read a few sentences then looked up at the captain in amazement.

"You're reading *Jane Eyre*?" he asked.

Captain Marrex nodded, then shrugged. "I asked S1N to find me a Human classic."

"And are you enjoying it?" Juniper asked, passing the tablet back. He'd read it when he first came aboard; no doubt S1N chose it because of that.

The captain looked down at the text, nodding again. "I haven't met many Humans before, and I was curious about your culture. However... I don't think I'm understanding something in the book."

"Well, I'd hardly call nineteenth-century England 'my' culture. You know, things have changed quite a bit over the last six centuries... but, what is it? Maybe I can explain."

The captain glanced up at him, then back down to the tablet. "Mr. Rochester is... rude to Jane. He's surly and peculiar. And..." Captain Marrex lifted his eyes again. "He's also... ugly.

However, Jane seems to like him, regardless of these things. Am I misreading it?"

Juniper smiled and shook his head. "No, I don't think you're misreading it. She *definitely* likes him."

"Why? He hasn't been very nice to her, and she barely knows him."

"Well... maybe she can see that there is a good man underneath all that. A lonely man. And she's interested in getting to know that part of him," Juniper said. If memory served him correctly, Rochester was a bit of a dick, but they weren't really talking about Jane and Mr. Rochester, were they? "Maybe he's only being rude to her because he's forgotten how to be any other way. *Maybe* he doesn't want to get his hopes up."

Captain Marrex stared at him for a few moments, his forehead creased, then snorted once in agreement. "Maybe." Though the Ghelyxian's facial physiognomy didn't really allow for smiling, Juniper thought his gaze had softened.

"You don't have any terrible secrets hiding in the attic, do you?" Juniper said in a playful tone.

"Why?" Captain Marrex said, sounding defensive again.

"Oh, I just meant... in the book..." he replied weakly.

"I haven't read about any terrible secrets yet."

"Oh. Well, I won't spoil it for you," Juniper said. "Sorry." He figured any second now, Captain Marrex would dismiss him. However, he was surprised when the captain spoke up in a quiet voice.

"I *do* have some secrets. They aren't particularly terrible, but... Would you like to hear them?"

Eagerly, Juniper nodded.

"I'm not an Imperial captain. This isn't really my ship."

"What?" Juniper sat forward, stunned. "But... *what?"*

"I came across the *Stellerion* shortly after I left my home world in disgrace. She was a derelict, drifting aimlessly outside

Imperial space," Captain Marrex answered. "The window to claim her expired; therefore, she's legally mine according to the Havian Charter."

"Do you know what happened?"

"A catastrophic systems failure killed everyone on board," said the Ghelyxian matter-of-factly.

Dismayed, Juniper looked down at his outfit. No wonder every room had closets full of clothes. He'd found it odd that so much had been left behind in what he'd *assumed* was a change of command.

"All right," he said calmly. "But why are you masquerading as an Imperial captain?"

Captain Marrex snorted and wrinkled his nose in what Juniper suddenly realized was the Ghelyxian version of a smile. "The uniform fit well enough, and I find it handy in business dealings."

"But the penalty for impersonating an Imperial officer is death."

"I know," replied the captain.

Juniper stared mutely at him. *He knows and doesn't care— what happened to you, Captain?*

The captain folded his arms on the table, leaning forward. "Juniper, what do you know about my species?"

Juniper pondered what he'd read about Ghelyxians. "Well... ah, you live on a ringed planet that has a tiny population, and your system of government is a monarchy... and Ghelyxians are considered the third-highest-ranking species in the Empire after the Hoch and The Elite."

Captain Marrex tapped his black claws on the table surface as he scrutinized Juniper. "Is that all?"

Juniper's face flushed, and he shook his head.

"It's all right... I won't bite. You know why I look the way I do?"

"If your species doesn't find a mate by the time puberty

starts, a genetic switch is thrown and your DNA becomes corrupted," Juniper answered quietly.

"You've done your reading." The captain picked up his cup of *leb* and took a sip, his pointed black tongue coming up to lick the white foam from his furry lip. "We call it 'the curse.' "

"Oh." Juniper frowned. "Is that why you left in disgrace? Because you're cursed?" He'd been frustrated by the lack of information on Ghelyxian culture in the database. There were numerous entries missing from every section—historical, social, political, even biological—and all the AIs could tell him was that the captain had been 'very angry' one day and erased part of it.

"On Ghelyx, commoners who are cursed must live out their lives in special reservations and are treated somewhat like the lepers of Old Earth's past. However, members of the royal family in the same condition are expected to commit their degraded bodies to the holy flame. In reality, there hasn't been a royal burned in generations. Instead, they're banished from the world itself and forbidden from entering Imperial space or having any dealings with Imperial entities," Captain Marrex said in a dry tone. "They're *effectively* dead because no one ever hears from them again."

Juniper could only stare at the captain for a few beats, eyes wide with the sudden conclusion his brain had leapt to.

"Holy shit... You're the prince, aren't you?"

The captain squinted at him, tilting his head. He wrinkled his nose. "Prince? Why not a lord or a duke?" he asked, sounding amused. "That's rather wild speculation."

"I read about dukes and barons and viscounts and whatever on Ghelyx, and just one *single* entry about a prince being born, which stuck out for me. It was strange because there should have been more about him, right? The birth of a prince or princess is cause for great celebration... but there is absolutely nothing mentioned of him ever again. No naming announcement and, if he died, no record of his death. He just... disappeared. *That's* what you deleted from the database, isn't it? *You.*"

Snorting, Captain Marrex nodded. "I hope you've never been accused of being slow."

Juniper smiled timidly. "No, sir. Um, Your Highness..."

"Just Marrex."

"All right... Marrex," Juniper said, liking the way the name felt on his tongue—he realized he'd never said it out loud before. For a bit, he just sat quietly, digesting what he'd learned while the captain gazed at him unblinking. "So," Juniper said at long last, "if you're a prince, why didn't you find a mate? I thought royal marriages were arranged?"

Marrex nodded. "They are, but my parents doted on me far more than they should have—I was their only child after what had been a very difficult gestation. Every eligible female and male was paraded in front of me, but I didn't think they were worthy. No one was ever attractive or intelligent enough for me. I was spoiled, vain, and arrogant. Any potential mate had to meet my ridiculous standards, and my parents kept indulging me... until it was too late. I woke up one morning and realized that I'd ignored the first signs of puberty. It was only a few days later that I started to degenerate. I kept it from them at first, but"—Marrex gave a low growl and turned to stare at his faint reflection in the viewport glass—"it's not something you can hide for very long."

"That's terrible," Juniper said, resting his chin on his hand. "They must have been devastated. I'm sorry."

Marrex turned back to Juniper with a bitter laugh. "Not devastated enough to let me stay." Closing his eyes, Marrex bowed his head for a moment. "But that's in the past. There's nothing I can do about it."

"Isn't there a cure? Treatment? Gene therapy?"

The captain lifted his head, shaking it. "Not once the change has started. There is actually a preventative—a treatment for children—but it's illegal. Ghelyxians value tradition over everything, even common sense."

"So, that means you're stuck as you are, even if you do find a mate?" Juniper asked quietly.

"Yes. I'm cursed to live out my life like this. Shunned and feared. In the underworld markets, do you know what I'm known as? Marrex the Monster."

Grimacing in sympathy, Juniper moved closer, taking the seat next to the captain.

Marrex stared at him, unmoving for a few seconds, then gave an angry-sounding snort. "Why are you *looking* at me like that?" Marrex growled. "How is it that you always *look* at me? Doesn't my ugliness repel you?"

Juniper shook his head firmly.

Marrex leaned closer and bared his fangs, but Juniper held his ground and placed his hand on Marrex's muscular forearm. The big Ghelyxian responded to the touch by freezing in place, his eyes comically wide.

"I don't think you're ugly," Juniper confessed.

"You... don't?"

"No." Juniper smiled. "Well, you *could* use a good brushing," he said, stroking the blood-red fur of Marrex's arm. "But ugly? Not at all."

"Is there something wrong with your eyes?" Marrex sounded incredulous. He stared down at Juniper's hand, his nostrils flaring, but he didn't move away.

"Nothing's wrong with my eyes. I just have different tastes than most men."

Marrex shook his head, his breathing a bit laboured, then he lifted his eyes to Juniper's and frowned, opened his mouth to say something else, closed it, then shook his head again. Slowly, he pulled his arm out of Juniper's grasp.

"What is it?" Juniper asked.

"I don't quite believe you."

"I guess I don't know if I would believe me either," he said. "But... believe me or not, it's your prerogative. I'm just telling it like it is."

After staring at Juniper for a moment longer, Marrex looked away, rising to his feet.

"It's getting late. Thank you for joining me for supper."

"Thank you for inviting me," Juniper replied, disappointed Marrex was already done with him—he'd hoped they'd keep talking. Juniper stared at the captain's broad back as he walked away. Well, that wasn't *all* he'd been hoping for.

A little jittery from the *leb*, Juniper wasn't ready to turn in yet. "Marrex," he said, and the Ghelyxian turned back to him with a questioning grunt. "Can I please call home?"

"Ah," Marrex said with a nod. "Of *course*."

"What is it?" Juniper asked, startled by the captain's cynical tone. *Damn.*

"Yes. Make the call. I don't care," Marrex said brusquely. "VAL can set up the encryption." He turned again and left the room.

"Thank you!" Juniper called after him, trying not to feel hurt over the abrupt end of the evening. He'd been hoping to leave it on a friendly note... not this cold dismissal. But at least he had permission to call his father.

A LITTLE WHILE LATER, Juniper wandered the corridors, arms wrapped around himself, waiting for VAL to finish whatever he was doing so that Juniper could make the call to Terra Deux. S1N walked silently at his side, glancing up at him from time to time. Finally, the AI broke the silence.

"So. You're a xenophile. That's interesting," S1N said conversationally.

Juniper frowned down at the cat.

"I really thought you were just buttering up the captain so you could call home," SIN continued. "But I saw your face... you really *are* hot for the boss, aren't you?"

"You were spying?"

"Of course, I was. You know this is just an interface, right? I'm actually everywhere all the time. Like God, only more charming," S1N replied, the tip of his tail twitching from side to side in time to his steps.

"Well, you're everywhere except for when you tried to figure out chicken noodle soup," Juniper pointed out with a grin.

"Embarrassing. Don't think I won't get back at you."

"But... what about VAL? He didn't know I was in the garden until I touched a flower and tripped the alarm. Isn't VAL everywhere too?"

"Dear VAL is pushing four hundred. He's an antique, really. Just like this ship. It'll be a wonder if VAL manages to get the long-range communicator to work. Captain Marrex only ever uses the short-range when he's looking to sell the junk we find."

"Oh," Juniper said softly.

"What is it?" S1N rose in the air until he was perched weightlessly on Juniper's shoulder.

"It's just really sad, that's all. The captain's been alone for so long."

"It's his own fault for being such an arrogant prat," said the AI.

"I know, but... he's suffered enough, don't you think?"

S1N paused with his pink tongue sticking out, his grooming interrupted. "I *do*, actually," he said gently. He fixed Juniper with his eyes narrowed. "Can I offer a piece of advice?"

"Sure."

"You know the captain thinks you only agreed to dine with him so you could make the call."

Juniper nodded. "I'm an idiot for bringing it up when I did."

"So—*don't make the call*. Not yet."

"What do you mean?"

"I mean, ask if you can join the captain for another meal. Put off calling your family for a while. They've been waiting seventeen years to hear from you... another few days or weeks won't make a difference, will it?"

Wrinkling his brow, Juniper pondered. "I guess they can wait." He nodded. Juniper really wanted to call home, but gaining the captain's trust had become important to him. "You're right. Thank you."

"Don't thank me yet," S1N said, jumping down to the floor.

Just then, VAL's shiny pale-blue face appeared in the air in front of Juniper, smiling wide. "It wasn't easy, but I have long-range communications online and I'm running an advanced encryption protocol on—"

"Thank you, but I'm not going to need it for now."

"What?" The AI's face went a sickly lime green, and the smile disappeared. "What happened? Did the captain change his mind? I'm certain I can ask him—"

"No, it's ok. Really. I'm just not ready to call them is all," Juniper said, trying to reassure the crestfallen AI. "But thank you, VAL. It's very much appreciated."

"You're welcome," VAL replied, sounding mystified.

"Actually, there *is* something you can do for me right now."

"Of course, Juniper. How can I help?"

"You can go find Juniper something really skimpy to wear," S1N said, and Juniper shot him a look of exasperation. The cat just stared back at him, his whiskers trembling with obvious amusement.

"VAL," Juniper said, turning back to the AI. "I would like you to ask Captain Marrex if he would do me the pleasure of dining with me tomorrow night."

MARREX STEPPED from the shadows as quietly as he could and knelt by Juniper's bed. In sleep, the Human looked utterly serene, something Marrex envied. Slowly, he reached out and moved a few strands of hair from Juniper's face, then held his breath when the young man's brow wrinkled. After a moment, his features smoothed out again, and Marrex sat back on his heels and sighed. Why would Juniper ask to dine with him again? It had to be a lie... a trick. But how could someone who slept so peacefully be so cruel?

Bowing his head, Marrex clenched his teeth against the mournful howl lodged in his chest, wishing he could ascertain Juniper's intentions. However, be they good or bad, Marrex knew was powerless to resist him.

CHAPTER 9
CONFESSIONS

Marrex stared at the bowl of soup in front of him, the warm steam rising from it fragrant and unfamiliar, though not unpleasant.

He lifted his eyes to the young man seated across from him, waiting for an explanation.

Juniper smiled and stirred his own soup. "It's chicken noodle soup."

With a grunt, Marrex picked up his spoon and prodded at the noodles floating in the broth. He carefully lifted a mouthful and slurped it. It was salty and vaguely meaty.

"So?" Juniper asked hopefully.

"Not bad," Marrex conceded, spooning up some more.

They'd been dining together for the last two weeks, taking turns choosing their communal meals. Though conversation was still somewhat stilted and awkward at times, Marrex found himself greatly looking forward to their times together. He eyed the young man as he tucked into his own bowl with enjoyment. Juniper had yet to contact his family, and that puzzled him... it was almost as if the young man honestly enjoyed Marrex's company.

This evening, Juniper was dressed in translucent yellow

69

silk that left little to the imagination. Earlier, when they had been standing, Marrex had had to force himself to stop trying to get glimpses of Juniper's obvious nudity beneath the yellow folds.

"You're quiet tonight," Juniper said.

Marrex grunted again and shrugged.

"What's wrong?"

Marrex mulled over what he was planning to say. He was unaccustomed to feeling so nervous.

"You can tell me," Juniper said, reaching across the table to lay his hand on Marrex's forearm.

As always, the fur at the back of Marrex's neck bristled at the touch. It was pure torture.

"You know," Juniper continued, a crease between his dark brows as he petted Marrex's arm, "maybe it's just the lighting in here but your fur looks... brighter than it used to." Juniper felt a few strands between his fingers, sending another shiver through Marrex. "But it's definitely softer."

Marrex had to clear his throat before speaking. "It... is?" He looked down at the red fur tufting between Juniper's long, slender fingers, and he swallowed. "I hadn't noticed."

"I'm sure of it. Have you changed your grooming habits?"

Marrex looked away, feeling foolishly embarrassed by the question. He *had* been taking more care...

"I'm sorry, was that too personal?" Juniper stopped ruffling Marrex's fur but didn't move his hand away.

"No. No. It's fine."

Smiling, Juniper tilted his head. "What is it? Come on... I know there's something you want to say."

Marrex snorted and frowned at Juniper. "There... is." He took a deep breath, looked up at the ceiling, then back down at Juniper. "Juniper... I need to apologize for something I've done."

"Oh? That sounds serious."

"I want to apologize for invading your privacy," Marrex

explained. "I've gone into your room a number of times while you were sleeping."

"Wow, that's not creepy *at all*," Juniper replied with a curl of his lip. He slid his hand off Marrex's arm. "I thought it was a cleaning drone that had taken that rose out of my room while I was asleep... It was you?"

Marrex nodded, ashamed of himself.

"How many times?"

"Eleven."

"*Why?*"

"The first time was to retrieve the rose. The rest..." Marrex blew out through his nostrils, shaking his head. "When I saw you sleeping there. You were so beautiful. So peaceful. I... have no excuse."

"You're right. That isn't an excuse."

"I know. Which is why I'm telling you now. I've betrayed your trust, and I don't expect you to forgive me, but you need to know what kind of... creature, I am." He couldn't bring himself to use the word *man*.

Arching one dark eyebrow, Juniper sat back and crossed his arms. "When? Were you there last night?"

"*No*," Marrex replied emphatically. "Not since our first dinner together. I promise."

"Why did you stop?"

"Because..." Marrex looked down at the tabletop, trying to put his thoughts into words, something which he was long out of practice with. "Because your feelings matter to me."

"Oh."

Marrex glanced up at Juniper and saw his expression had gone shrewd.

"Are you interested in making it up to me?" Juniper asked.

Relief uncoiled the knots in Marrex's chest, and he nodded quickly. "Yes. Of course."

"Walk with me in your garden."

For a moment, Marrex could only stare. He thought it was a good thing that his face hid his emotions well, otherwise Juniper might have recoiled from the knee-jerk anger that boiled up at the thought of sharing his sacred space... but then he mentally took a step back and wondered why it was such an affront. Would it be such a terrible thing to let Juniper in? He sighed, thinking about the complete solitude that never seemed to lessen his misery.

"All right."

Juniper walked quietly beside Marrex as they took the winding path through the garden. As they had last time, the warm, fragrant air and lush plants filled him to the brim with joy. He wanted to touch the velvety soft petals of a large purple rose as they passed it or to run his hand over the frilly ferns along the path, but he kept his arms at his side, not wanting to provoke the captain in any way. He could tell how anxious Marrex was, sharing this space of his.

Eventually, their leisurely pace took them to the stone bench and the small statue on its pedestal. Juniper couldn't help but smile to himself over the many times he'd been here in his dreams, but then he sobered, remembering the conclusion of those dreams.

"Marrex?"

The captain grunted, looking over at him.

"The symbols carved into the door... what do they mean?" he asked gently.

Marrex snorted and tossed his head, and Juniper saw he had balled his fists, but he stayed silent, waiting for the captain to answer.

Finally, Marrex let out a long sigh and shrugged. "Here lies Marrex the Monster." He gave a bitter little laugh and sat down on the bench, clasping his hands between his knees. "I was..." He swallowed twice as if repulsed by his thoughts. "I was at a very low point."

Juniper nodded. "I can understand."

"Can you?" Marrex asked, tilting his head up to appraise Juniper. His black eyes bored into Juniper, but there was no malice in them, just weariness.

"I left the only home I ever knew to board a colony ship just so my family wouldn't be forced to live hand to mouth. Basically, I exiled myself... I know it's not what happened to you, but I was feeling really low knowing I'd probably never see them again."

Marrex grunted. Then he surprised Juniper by gesturing to the bench.

Grateful and a bit nervous, Juniper sat down next to Marrex. The bench wasn't all that big so their thighs touched, and Juniper felt a little heat rise up his neck and into his cheeks.

After clearing his throat, Marrex motioned to the foliage in front of them. "Some of these plants were already here before I came aboard the *Stellerion*," the big Ghelyxian explained in a quiet voice. "Once I'd disposed of the bodies of the crew and made adequate repairs to the ship, this became my sanctuary. I worked on it for many years, adding plants and trees when I could. It brought me peace." Marrex let out a slow breath, glancing around. "But the solitude became oppressive. It was the silence of a grave... and then I knew this place would become that one day—my grave." Looking over at the small statue, Marrex shook his head. "I used to look like that, you know."

"I figured. Did you carve it?"

"I did, actually," Marrex looked down at his hands. "They might be deformed now, but they are still useful."

Juniper reached over and took one of Marrex's hands in his, running his fingers over the large furry knuckles. Then he turned it over and discovered Marrex's palm felt like velvet or suede. Lifting Marrex's hand to his face, Juniper smiled at the captain's dazed look.

"I see nothing wrong with your hands," Juniper said, rubbing his cheek against the soft palm. "They're strong and warm."

Marrex's nostrils flared, and the tip of his black tongue touched his top lip for a second before disappearing. He looked terrified, and Juniper thought it was funny that he could make a beast of a man like Marrex as nervous as a virgin.

Juniper rose up off the bench, knowing full well he was completely on display through the gauzy yellow silk he was wearing.

"What... are you doing?" breathed Marrex.

"We should dance," Juniper replied, pulling on Marrex's hand.

"We should?" Marrex rose slowly, his black eyes wide. "There's no music."

"S1N?" Juniper called out. Immediately, some slow music started playing over the intercom system.

For a moment, Marrex only stared at him. Then he gave Juniper a slow, formal bow before extending his free arm in a curve to invite Juniper to step into his embrace.

Tilting his head, Juniper chuckled. "You can dance?"

"Probably better than you," Marrex replied, lifting his chin. "I'm a prince, after all."

"Touché." Juniper smiled and let Marrex take him in his arms, then he frowned. "Hey, why do you assume *you're* going to lead?"

Marrex just growled and pulled him closer, swaying them to the music.

"You know, you're not as big of a grouch as you make yourself out to be," Juniper said softly.

74

"Hm." Marrex looked down at him and wrinkled his nose in a smile.

The captain's body was warm and solid against Juniper's, and though Juniper was shorter than Marrex, owing to the differences in their species, their hips were about level. Gradually, the lights dimmed in the garden until they were the blue of early dusk. Juniper sighed and leaned his head against Marrex's shoulder, and he felt Marrex's arm tighten around his waist as their dance slowed. He pulled Marrex's hand back to his cheek to nuzzle it again and heard a low rumble come from Marrex's broad chest.

"I don't like that you broke into my room to watch me sleep," Juniper said, running Marrex's hand down the side of his neck. "But I *do* like that you think I'm beautiful." His heart was pounding loud enough that it was like a drum in his ears. Juniper looked up. Marrex just stared at him unblinking, his palm trembling against Juniper's neck.

"I dream about you," Juniper confessed.

"You do?" Marrex's voice was hoarse.

"Almost every night." He brought Marrex's hand down lower and coaxed it into a loose fist so that he could run the captain's knuckles over his nipple.

Marrex's back straightened, and he let out a raspy little groan.

"Do you still have any doubts that I'm attracted to you?" Juniper asked, cocking his head. He wondered if Marrex could feel how fast his pulse was going.

First, Marrex began to nod, but then he stopped, bared his fangs in a grimace, and shrugged.

Laughing, Juniper shook his head and pushed his pelvis against the captain's, causing the Ghelyxian's eyes to widen.

"See?" Juniper whispered. He pulled back a little so he could guide Marrex's unresisting hand down his front to the unambiguous silken tent. "Feel how hard you make me."

Finding his hand atop Juniper's erection seemed to shake Marrex out of his stupor. He let out a low growl and wrapped his hand around Juniper's shaft. Juniper gasped and closed his eyes as the captain fondled him gently through the silk.

"You feel so good," Juniper whispered. Curling his hand around the back of Marrex's thick neck, he threaded his fingers through the coarse fur, sighing with pleasure as Marrex's caresses became rougher.

Marrex chuckled softly, and he said, "I haven't done this for a long time."

Juniper felt the tips of Marrex's claws press into him, and he shivered, letting out a low moan. "Yeah, me neither," he murmured, wincing in a mix of pleasure and pain.

Marrex let out a roar of a laugh, and Juniper nearly jumped out of his skin at the suddenness of it. Then he realized that his seventeen years was nothing compared to Marrex's hundred and twelve.

He looked up at Marrex with a grin. "Right. You have me beat there." Juniper exhaled sharply as Marrex squeezed him harder. "Oh god, that's good."

"Yes?"

"Oh *yes*." He looked down and saw that Marrex's claws had made small rips in the yellow silk—he couldn't wait to feel how Marrex's soft palm felt against his naked cock.

"You're an interesting creature, Juniper Bo," Marrex said, sounding amused. "How do you even know we're compatible?"

"We'll figure it out," replied Juniper, gritting his teeth as Marrex clutched his backside with the other hand, his claws digging in.

"What do you want me to do?"

Juniper cleared his throat and smiled. "I want you to take off your shirt."

Marrex's hand froze midstroke, Juniper's request obviously catching him off guard.

"Please?" Juniper added, searching the Ghelyxian's pupilless eyes.

"As you wish," Marrex replied begrudgingly, releasing Juniper.

Juniper sat back down on the bench to watch Marrex tackle the buttons on the front of his blue dress shirt. Slowly, they came apart, and when Marrex pulled the shirt out of his pants to take it off completely, Juniper could only stare.

"Wow," he said in total awe.

Marrex had broad, powerful shoulders and flat pectorals with no nipples, and his abdomen was a horizontally striated mass of muscle with no navel. The entirety of his torso was covered in the same blood-red fur he had on his face and arms, thicker and longer across his chest but from his sternum to where his pelvis disappeared beneath the black pants, the fur was shorter with a central line of darker patterns that reminded Juniper of Rorschach inkblots. He wondered if the captain's cock would have the same black butterfly pattern he had seen in his dreams.

"These marks," Marrex said, ruffling the dark patterns on his belly. "They are part of my... curse."

"I don't care. I think they're beautiful."

Head cocked, Marrex stared hard at Juniper as if trying to gauge his sincerity, so Juniper spread his knees apart and beckoned to him with both hands. "Come here."

Marrex stepped forward, but when Juniper reached for the buttoned front of his trousers, Marrex grabbed his wrists.

"If you're going to tell me you're deformed or ugly or cursed or whatever again, you can stop there," Juniper said, gazing up at Marrex. "You're not going to scare me off... I want to see you. *All* of you. Please?"

Again, the word brought another reticent nod from Marrex, and he let go of Juniper's arms.

Hands shaking slightly from anticipation, Juniper undid

the buttons on Marrex's pants, then slowly pulled them open. Below the hard-muscled, furry abdomen, the line of dark patterns continued until they surrounded the root of his thick, half-hard cock. Like his palms, Marrex's shaft was covered in very short velvety fur, but as Juniper slid the captain's pants down further, he saw the head was smooth and hairless. He smiled when he saw the black stripes and butterfly.

"What?" Marrex growled.

"I'm just... sometimes I wonder if I'm still asleep, dreaming in my stasis pod," Juniper admitted.

"What do you mean?"

"I just mean... I don't know what I mean." Juniper laughed. "It's just too perfect." Maybe all Ghelyxians had the same cockhead pattern, and he'd seen it somewhere in his research. He'd look it up later. Juniper looked back up and smiled. "What do *you* want me to do?" He licked his lips.

However, Marrex was the one to sink to his knees in front of Juniper, and without any effort, the Ghelyxian quickly tore apart the rest of the damp yellow silk covering Juniper's erection. Marrex snorted, his breath hot on Juniper's skin, and he looked into Juniper's eyes as his black tongue snaked out and licked his cock from root to tip.

"Holy *fuck*," Juniper moaned, leaning back so the captain's horns wouldn't rake him. "Do that again."

Marrex chuckled, then obliged him, taking his time to cover every part of his cock with his smooth, wet tongue, teasingly resting his furry lips open on the swollen crown as if he would take Juniper into his mouth, but then retreating to lick hot traces down the shaft again.

Juniper's thighs quivered, and he reached out to grasp Marrex by the lower horns to stop him after his serpentine tongue wound its way entirely around the base of Juniper's cockhead.

"S... stop," Juniper said, his breathing out of control. "Hang on. *Wow*."

Marrex tried to move his head, his tongue squeezing Juniper's shaft harder, but Juniper held fast. Then, the unimaginable happened—one of Marrex's glossy black horns came away from his head with a loud *crack*. Immediately, Juniper released the captain, staring in horror at the heavy horn in his hand.

"Oh my god. I am so sorry," Juniper said. "I didn't know that could happen. I was just worried I wasn't going to be able to hold back and I never thought to look up whether that could be poisonous to your species and oh man, I hope I didn't hurt you... I am *so* sorry," he said in a panic.

Marrex felt the smooth spot where the horn had been and frowned. "That shouldn't have happened." He took the horn from Juniper and examined the base. Then, he reached up and took hold of the opposite horn, giving it a hard yank. It too broke off in Marrex's hand.

"What are you *doing*?" Juniper asked, aghast.

"My species has two horns. Only the cursed grow a second pair," Marrex said quietly. "I wonder..."

"What?"

"It's... nothing. I'm fine," replied the captain. Then he set aside the horns and fixed Juniper with a narrow-eyed gaze. "And it's not."

"What's not... *uhh*," Juniper threw his head back as Marrex took his nipples between his fingers and twisted lightly.

"Not poisonous," Marrex said in a low growl. Once more the captain's long tongue wound its way around Juniper's cock, but this time it was to pull it deep into his mouth.

Juniper let out a cry as Marrex began to treat him to the most thorough blow job in his decidedly generous experience. Either Ghelyxians had extra muscles in their mouths or their tongues were more than just flexible, but Juniper felt as if his wet cock was being stroked in opposite directions while being simultaneously squeezed and licked. Every time Marrex's fangs touched his cockhead, Juniper was sure he was going to shoot his load, but somehow, he managed to hold back longer.

"I want you," he rasped. "Marrex, please..."

The captain pulled back slowly, giving Juniper's cock another enveloping lick, and frowned up at him. Silently, Marrex stood, gathering Juniper up in his strong arms, and Juniper wrapped his legs around the captain's waist, bestowing a kiss first on his furry cheek, then to the side of his mouth, and finally, gingerly, he kissed him on the lips. Juniper's backside rested in the captain's hands, and Marrex squeezed his cheeks through what remained of the silk as he opened up to the kiss. Marrex's mouth tasted slightly peppery, and his smooth tongue curled playfully around Juniper's as they kissed. After a few moments, Marrex drew his head back, his nose wrinkled in what Juniper took as a smirk.

"Kissing is not something Ghelyxians do," he explained. "But I think I like it."

"Oh?" said Juniper, breathless. His head was spinning.

Sobering, Marrex gazed at him. "Do you really want me, Juniper?"

It was obvious that the captain was talking about more than just sex, and for a moment, Juniper was struck dumb. He hadn't really thought that far ahead. Sex, sure... but did he really want to commit himself to someone who'd been alone for so long? Someone who was so quick to take offense to every perceived slight?

Did Juniper really want someone with that much baggage? Maybe he was just reading too much into the question...

"Juniper?" Marrex murmured.

Juniper stared into Marrex's black eyes, full of hope and dread... and saw himself reflected in them. He placed his hands softly to each side of Marrex's furry face, and he sighed.

"I *think* so," Juniper said quietly.

Marrex's nostrils widened as he took a quick breath, and a wrinkle appeared on his brow. He was disappointed, that was obvious. However, when Juniper pulled Marrex's face closer for a kiss, he felt the captain's eagerness return—Marrex's hands squeezed his backside more firmly, the eight points of his claws sharp.

Juniper shivered and groaned as Marrex broke the kiss to begin biting the side of his neck. "Harder," he whispered, then let out a soft cry as Marrex obliged him. The captain's fangs would leave marks on him, but Juniper didn't think he would break the skin unless asked.

Slowly, Marrex bent at the waist, supporting Juniper's weight easily, and set him down gently on his back on the short mosslike grass. When Marrex stood again, it was to pull off his black boots and take his pants down the rest of the way, revealing thick muscular thighs and calves, his knees dark like the patterns down his chest, and large clawed feet.

Juniper smiled and shook his head. Marrex looked like a demon out of some twisted fairy tale and that suited him just fine. His eyes lingered on the captain's big cock. Unlike Humans, Ghelyxians had internal testes and their shafts were much wider at the base than the slim head, but it was a beautiful sight. He watched a clear drop fall from the lower slit to the grass and exhaled in eagerness.

"You're torturing me," he said, fondling his own achingly hard dick. "Please?"

Marrex tilted his head but said nothing, lowering himself to his knees between Juniper's thighs, his cock drooling another clear drop onto Juniper's belly.

"I don't see how this is going to work," Marrex said, staring down at himself. "I'm going to hurt you."

Reaching for Marrex's erection, Juniper gave it a few

coaxing strokes. It *was* big. Really big. But that just excited him more.

"It'll be fine. Trust me. I've taken a fist before, so this should be a piece of cake."

Marrex recoiled and held up his fist, looking at it—it was about the size of Juniper's head.

Laughing, Juniper shook his head. "Human fist."

"Why?" Marrex sounded mildly horrified.

"Because I wanted to. And it felt great, trust me." Juniper beckoned to Marrex. "Come here... I just want to feel you on me for a bit, then I'll run to a replicator and see about making some lube. We're going to need a *lot* of it."

"We have it already," Marrex replied. "See?" He moved Juniper's fingers to the bottom of his cock, right between the two black bands. Juniper could feel hard lumps beneath the wet velvet of the shaft. Slowly, Marrex pressed his fingers into the lumps and a thick ribbon of the clear liquid, something Juniper had assumed was similar to precum, shot out of the bottom slit in Marrex's cockhead and splashed down on him, covering his groin and hand, warm and slippery.

"Wow," Juniper said.

"Special glands," Marrex said in a husky voice. His eyes were on Juniper's hand fondling himself, and his breathing was deep and measured. "I'll go slow."

Nodding, Juniper spread his knees further, holding onto the backs of this thighs. His pulse was swift and light, as if his heart were beating too fast to push enough blood through his system, and he realized he was scared—but that was part of the allure. However, when Marrex finally started pushing his cock against Juniper's pucker, Juniper let out a cry and shoved at Marrex's hips.

"Wait... w-wait wait... Oh god. Hang on." Immediately, Marrex froze, and Juniper panted a few jittery breaths. "Just try not to impale me, ok?"

"We can stop."

"Not on your life."

Chuckling, Marrex leaned down and kissed Juniper softly on the lips. "All right. Ready?"

Juniper nodded.

When the head of Marrex's cock breached the tight ring of muscle, Juniper tensed, the pain sharp for a moment, and then he let out a few short breaths. "Ok. More."

Marrex grunted and thrust, causing Juniper to gasp and grit his teeth. "Fuck. Ow... oh god... that *hurts*," he said, his voice breaking. "But... oh *fuck*... the good kind. Go on."

Looking at him questioningly for a moment, Marrex's big chest heaved with his breathing, his nostrils flared and fangs bared, and then he resumed, bit by bit, forcing his huge shaft into Juniper's body, pausing at Juniper's whimpers and wails of protest. However, when Marrex hit a second sphincter or a bend when he wasn't more than halfway in, Juniper yelped and dug his nails into Marrex's thighs.

"Stop!"

Again, Marrex stopped moving, and Juniper lay there for a moment with his eyes closed.

"Ok, go... slow as you can," Juniper whispered. He put his hands on his belly and thought he could feel the bulge as Marrex penetrated him deeper. Juniper's cock, which had softened considerably, perked up at the idea, and he let out a shaky breath.

Marrex began thrusting his hips, not going much deeper but working up to a rhythm that had Juniper moaning and pushing up his own hips in eagerness. That's when he noticed a warm tingling sensation that spread from his ass all the way to his extremities, making him a bit dizzy, like he'd just taken a hit of some kind of drug. It felt good, but he frowned, shaking his head to try to rid himself of it. The pleasure just increased, getting stronger until it felt like his dick was a hot, throbbing pulsar.

"What the... I think something is wro—Oh *god*," Juniper yelled, not able to finish his thought before his balls let loose and his cock blasted cum onto his chest. Marrex let out a low moan and quickened his pace a bit, curling his hands around Juniper's waist as Juniper trembled and twitched, groaning with each sublime volley, lost in the blistering climax that throbbed through his entire body.

When Juniper could breathe again, he let out a weak laugh, inwardly cursing himself for getting off so easily... then he realized that instead of subsiding after the peak, he was about to climax again.

Through clenched teeth, Juniper grunted and thrust his hips, emptying his balls a second time. Again, there was no relief, just a swift climb right back up to the pinnacle of orgasm. He came a third time with a yell and shook his head. "Marrex... there's something... *ahhh fuuuuuckkk*," Juniper groaned as his body was pulsing and twitching through another orgasm. "I-think-I'm-having-a"—Juniper let out a sob as another exquisite wave of pleasure crashed through him—"reaction-to-whatever-is-in-your... *huhh*." He was covered in sweat and trembling like a leaf as he continued to climax over and over again.

"It's just a stimulant," Marrex said, thrusting faster again. "It's harmless."

"Harm... *lessssss fuck*," Juniper gasped, his whole body throbbing through another orgasm.

"Should I stop?"

"N-no... *no!*" Juniper almost screamed as he came hard again, tears flowing freely down his cheeks. He could barely see, and it felt like his entire groin was electrified and throbbing, but not with any pain. Juniper gasped and moaned through yet another climax, and another, his dick just going through the motions, long spent of any cum left in his body. He wondered if it was possible to die of pleasure.

Marrex let out a harsh sound, his claws scraping Juniper's sides, and he went perfectly still though Juniper could feel the pulses in his stretched-out sphincter... which sent him into yet another full-body orgasm. This time he could only mewl softly as he wept and shuddered. Finally, Marrex pulled out and lay down beside him, pulling him into his arms. Juniper only barely registered that the captain's sweat smelled like a cross between cloves and black pepper, because even though Marrex had stopped fucking him, another wave swept over him, leaving him twitching and clutching at the captain.

"Are you all right?" Marrex asked, sounding breathless and amused.

"I think... that went... rather well," Juniper rasped, then promptly passed out.

JUNIPER WOKE up in his room, naked and alone in his bed. He rubbed his eyes and whispered, "S1N?"

There was a static crackle, and the cat appeared on the pillow next to his head, staring down at him with whiskers trembling.

"You called, lover boy?"

"What time is it? What happened?"

"You passed out," S1N answered, turning around once to curl into a ball with his nose only inches away from Juniper's. He yawned. "And it's late."

"Passed out from what? Did I have some kind of allergic reaction to Marrex?"

"No. Just sheer exhaustion. And by my scans, you're still needing another few hours. So... close your eyes and go back to sleep, Human."

Juniper continued to lie there, staring at the ceiling. He was sore just about everywhere, like he'd had one hell of a workout. His abdomen was probably the worst... he felt like he'd done a thousand crunches. No doubt it was from tensing and writhing through all those orgasms. Juniper frowned and gingerly cupped his balls. They were swollen and tender to the touch.

"Were you watching?" he asked S1N.

"Unfortunately."

"Could you tell how many times I came?" Juniper winced as he shifted to investigate his ass, and found himself sore but not overly bruised which was surprising.

"Thirty-seven times," S1N replied.

"Holy shit," Juniper said, laughing. Then he clutched his abs and groaned. "Ow. Can I get a painkiller?"

VAL appeared in the air above him, his slightly transparent face a swirl of lavender and lilac.

"Of course, you can, but it will take approximately fifteen minutes for the delivery droid to get here. Conversely, you can get up and go get it yourself in five."

Juniper gave an exasperated sigh. "That's it. I'm going to install a replicator in my room."

"The captain has a distribution port in *his* room," S1N said and started purring, his eyes closed. "Why not move in with him?"

"Um. I don't know about that," Juniper said. He tried to sit up but decided it wasn't worth it and flopped back on the bed. "Fine... Send the droid." He looked over at S1N. "We had sex— that doesn't automatically mean I should just move in." He rubbed his face. "Besides, he hasn't asked me to."

"And he probably won't... I don't know if you noticed, but our crotchety captain is a bit of shrinking violet when it comes to his affection for you," S1N said. "You're the one who put the moves on *him*, remember?"

"Hm" was all Juniper replied, and then he narrowed his eyes, spotting something on the table next to his bed. It was a long-stemmed rose in a narrow vase, the flower bright blue at its heart with blue so dark it was almost black edging the petals. Juniper smiled at the beautiful gift. "He really does like me, doesn't he?" he asked quietly.

"I can tell you that right now he's sitting up in bed reading, but he hasn't flipped a page in a long time. His heart rate is elevated, and his pleasure hormones are unusually high. I can't read his mind, of course, but I'd bet my whiskers he's thinking about you," S1N replied.

Juniper closed his eyes with a grin and let out a long happy sigh. He wasn't sure exactly how he felt about Marrex, not yet anyway, but he definitely wanted another go at that magic dick of his. Though, perhaps he should look up how to counter the effect it had on him—at least a *little*. He didn't know if he'd survive another thirty-seven straight orgasms.

Chuckling, Juniper shook his head and winced. He was getting horny again just thinking about it, but his body was a wreck.

"How much longer until the droid gets here?"

"Twelve minutes."

With another irked sigh, Juniper folded his hands over his chest, resigned to wait.

It was nice that Marrex hadn't just assumed and taken him to his own bed to recover—Juniper had never been a stay-over kind of guy, more like a that-was-fun, I'll-call-you-maybe kind of guy—but the more he thought about it, the more he felt a little disappointed that he hadn't woken up to that great big furry body next to him.

CHAPTER 10
CUT TO THE CHASE

Marrex was twiddling one of the toggles on his armchair, his mind circling the Human as it had nonstop since they'd coupled the day before. What was Juniper doing right now? Was he reading? Eating breakfast? Choosing one of his eccentric outfits?

Is he thinking about me?

Growling low over the silliness of his thoughts, Marrex shook his head, then frowned. That was interesting too—he was still unused to how light his head felt without his secondary horns. Marrex lifted his hand and looked closely at his fur. It was definitely brighter, and the nail beds of his claws were smoother, more like they had been before his change. Did he dare hope that somehow his interactions with Juniper had reversed some of his transformation?

"Marrex?" came Juniper's voice, startling the captain out of his thoughts.

Marrex looked over at the door and stood in the same motion, nearly stumbling in his haste. "Hello," he replied.

Juniper's hair was wet and hung loose over his shoulders. Today he was wearing a pale-blue poncho over a pair of glittery silver leggings and his feet were bare like usual.

"Can I come in?" Juniper asked. "Or... is it 'on'? Can I come *on* to the bridge? How do you say it?"

"Doesn't matter," Marrex replied, then realized he sounded curt and cleared his throat. "I mean: whichever you prefer. And yes, please do."

With a soft chuckle, Juniper stepped through the doorway. "Thank you."

"How... are you?" Marrex asked, wishing he knew what to do with his arms. Did he cross them? Put his hands on his hips? Never before had his arms felt completely superfluous.

"Good," Juniper replied. "You?"

"Good... you?"

Marrex grimaced when he realized he'd already asked him that. Juniper groaned and rubbed his face, shaking his head.

"*What?*" Marrex growled, hunching his shoulders defensively.

Juniper came closer and looked up at Marrex, his big brown eyes serious. "Let's just get something out of the way, ok? I hate it when it gets all awkward... Marrex, I *really* enjoyed last night. I had the time of my life. I only wish I wasn't so sore this morning because I would throw you down right here and now and ride the hell out of that gorgeous dick of yours."

Marrex was so startled that he could do nothing but stare at the young man for a few seconds, and then he began to laugh. Juniper grinned up at him.

"You like that?" Juniper asked. "I prefer cutting right to the chase."

"It's... refreshing," Marrex replied.

"Now your turn."

Marrex opened his mouth, then closed it. He shook his head and tried again.

"I... ah. Hm."

"You're going to have to do better than that." Juniper smirked.

"I'm not used to talking. Period."

"Were you never much of a conversationalist, or is it because you've been sulking all by yourself in this crypt of a spaceship for so long?"

Sulking? Marrex was about to argue but stopped himself. After all, it was true.

Juniper searched his eyes, his cheeks a little pink. "Did I just overstep?"

"No." Marrex placed a hand on Juniper's shoulder and squeezed. "Here." He backed up, pulling Juniper with him, and sat down in his captain's chair. Patting his lap, he said, "Up."

Grinning, Juniper turned around and sat down on Marrex's thighs, and when Marrex put his arms around him, he sighed and leaned back against his chest.

Marrex brought his face close to the side of Juniper's neck and sniffed his skin, causing Juniper to giggle and squirm.

"What... what are you *doing*?" Juniper said, letting out another peal of laughter when Marrex snuffled him again.

"I'm smelling you," the captain murmured. "You're beautiful to look at, but just as beautiful to smell. My species has a great appreciation for scent."

"Oh." Juniper craned his head to the side to accommodate Marrex's slow perusal of his neck. He stifled another giggle. "Sorry, I'm ticklish."

"Mm."

"What do I smell like?"

"You smell like *you*... it's hard to explain—there aren't really words for it in your language."

"That's too bad. Maybe I should learn yours."

Marrex snorted in amusement. "I don't know if I'd bother if I were you. It's far harder to learn than your tongue."

"That's something I've been meaning to ask: how *do* you speak it so well?"

"I'm of royal blood... I speak a number of languages. And

what I lacked in fluency when I came aboard the *Stellerion*, I soon made up for in practice—I couldn't find a way to change the language settings on her interfaces. The ship was an Imperial delegation transport so everything was locked to Imperial Standard."

Marrex heard S1N chuckle to himself from above the viewscreen where he was curled up.

"My ears were ringing for months from all the Ghelyxian cursing. It's not a pretty language to listen to with even the *nice* words..." said the AI, stretching out his front paws. "I thought VAL was going to have a breakdown."

The captain ignored S1N and slid his hands up under Juniper's loose poncho to pull it up. Juniper obliged and lifted his arms so Marrex could take it all the way off. Breathing in deep, he ran his palms over Juniper's bare shoulders, pecs, then belly, smiling when Juniper's scent took on distinct notes of arousal.

Juniper let out a moan as Marrex nibbled at his neck, and S1N sat up, his fur bristling.

"Oh god. Get a room," the AI muttered and vanished.

Juniper's chuckle was interrupted when Marrex whacked him with his horn as he bent down to kiss his shoulder. "Ow!" Juniper said, rubbing the side of his head.

"Sorry. Like I said... we don't really kiss. Now I think I know why," Marrex said ruefully.

"Like *I* said... We'll figure it out," the young man replied. "With lots of practice."

"All right." Though his tone didn't sound it, Marrex was deliriously happy that Juniper wanted him. The most beautiful Human he'd ever seen... and he *wanted* Marrex. *Lots of practice indeed...* Though he didn't know if Juniper's feelings for him could ever run deep, Marrex knew he could be very happy just with the physical aspect. At least for a little while.

The captain licked the side of Juniper's neck and circled his nipple with his foreclaw, making the young man shiver, but then Juniper shook his head and just pressed Marrex's hand against his breast.

"I am *way* too sore for anything, you beast," Juniper murmured, stroking the fur on Marrex's arm.

"What would you like me to do then?"

"Just hold me. I'd like that a lot."

Wrapping his arms around Juniper, Marrex smiled. "As you wish."

CHAPTER II
CALLING HOME

Arms behind his head, Juniper lay in bed watching Marrex get dressed. "Why do you bother?" he asked. "I'm just going to undress you the first chance I get."

Marrex looked up from buttoning his trousers with an amused expression. Over the last month, the Ghelyxian's coarse fur had mostly fallen out, replaced by fur that was glossy and very short everywhere but his chest. Though the patterns down his front had stayed nearly black, the rest of him was now the exact same shade of brilliant red as the Ferrari Cloudshredder from the early twenty-fourth-century remake of *Ferris Bueller's Day Off*.

"You're so sexy," Juniper said with a shrug. "I just can't help myself."

"You're insatiable," Marrex replied and resumed buttoning, a task that was easier for him now that his claws were shorter.

Sometimes Juniper sort of missed how sharp the Ghelyxian's claws had been, but he didn't miss the stitches he'd needed after one particularly hot and heavy tangle with the captain.

"Do you want me to get up with you?" Juniper asked, not really wanting to. The captain's huge bed was *far* more

95

comfortable than the one in Juniper's quarters—not that he'd spent any time in his own bed in weeks.

"No. Stay. I'm just going to take another look at that derelict ship VAL spotted yesterday." Marrex walked towards the door, but he paused at the threshold and looked back over his shoulder. "You're going to call them today?"

Juniper nodded. Why did he feel so damn guilty about it? "I've put it off long enough," he said. "I have to let them know I'm alive."

"All right," Marrex said, his voice strangely tight.

"I'll come see you afterwards."

With a nod, Marrex left.

JUNIPER SMILED as the image came through, grainy and stuttering because of the weak connection—Terra Deux was obviously besieged by heavy solar flares—but clear enough that he could easily see the last seventeen years on his older sister's face. She'd always been spare, but pretty in a waiflike sort of way. She was still attractive, but maturity had made her features more distinct, and her gaze had the shrewdness of someone who'd lived a hard life.

"Acacia?" Juniper said when the woman hadn't spoken.

"What is this?" Acacia asked, bringing her face closer to the camera. "Who are you?"

"It's Juniper."

For a moment, it looked like Acacia was going to refute his claim, but her eyes widened, searching his face. "Juniper?"

"Hi."

"Oh my god. Juniper! How... where...." she stammered, lifting a hand to her mouth to stare at him for a few long seconds.

"How are you?" he asked.

"Oh my god, you're *alive*..." Acacia said and looked over her shoulder. "Peggy, go get Willow."

"Who's Peggy?"

"Peggy's my daughter. Your niece, I guess. Hold on, how are you *alive*? Tell me that first. I can't believe I'm looking at you." She turned away again and shouted, "I don't know! Try the cellar." Then she stared at Juniper again. "And you're young. How are you so *young*?"

"Well, I spent seventeen years in stasis... I was found in a wrecked Nelami shuttlecraft. The rest is a mystery."

Acacia's grainy face moved over to make way for a much plumper and older version of the Willow he remembered.

"Juniper!" Willow nearly screamed. "Oh my god. Is that really you?"

"Hi."

"How is it possible? Oh my god... and you're so young, you little shit," Willow continued with a raspy laugh.

"Stasis," Juniper explained.

"He was picked up by the Nelami," Acacia said, squeezing back into the picture.

"What the hell would the Nelami do with Juniper?"

"How should I know? Maybe they were hoping to sell him at one of those horrible pleasure moons? Or maybe they wanted him for themselves. Juniper always *did* attract the freaks and—"

"Hey, I'm right here," Juniper said, annoyed. "Where's Dad?"

Acacia and Willow both stared at him for a moment, and Acacia's brows met over her long nose. "Juniper... They lost contact with the colony ship less than a day out from Rhesh-14. Blackskimmers were sent out to find wreckage, anything, but they found no trace of it. Everyone figured the ship ran into pirates or somehow got off course and crashed. There were many theories—"

"Yeah, oh god, there was one about the Krem shipbuilders

purposefully outfitting colony ships with faulty navigational systems so they could populate some giant star weapon against—"

"Oh, Willow, you're such a twit... no one believes that and—"

"Hey!" Juniper said, interrupting their bickering. He leaned closer to the camera. "So *where is Dad*?"

Acacia and Willow shared a glance.

"Dad took it really hard when they stopped the search," Willow said gently. "He started standing outside, staring at the sky—without a suit. You remember what that's like? He'd just burn to a crisp and then be in the hospital for weeks. But he'd do it again as soon as he was out. His mind... it just sort of..." She snapped her fingers and shrugged.

"What Willow is trying to say is that Dad is not well," Acacia said. "Mentally and physically... he's not the same man you remember. He's just a shell."

Juniper stared at the grainy image, his heart pounding and mouth dry. He blinked a few times to try to keep his tears from falling, but they slid down his cheeks. "I'm coming home," he said.

"Oh, Juny... honey..." Willow said, glancing over at Acacia. "If you do... um... we can't really afford to feed you for long. I'm sorry. We're stretched as thin as molimfibre here."

"But, if you had a little money," Acacia said, side-eyeing Willow. "To help out with medical expenses..."

"Whatever it takes," Juniper said, shaking his head. "I'll figure out something. I just have to—" He remembered that Marrex was barred from Imperial space... but maybe the captain cared enough for him to risk it... *and* lend him money. "I'll come home as soon as I can."

MARREX CLOSED HIS EYES, enjoying the vigorous brushing Juniper was giving him. Though the bright-red fur on his face and arms was once again short and smooth and didn't require that much grooming, Juniper insisted on taking care of the thick, tapering crest of fur down his chest. Not that Marrex was complaining, of course—it felt so good that if he wasn't so cocksore and utterly spent, he'd be tempted to see if Juniper could be coaxed into another quick coupling.

Smiling, Marrex snorted and opened his eyes. Not that Juniper needed much coaxing—he'd never met anyone as voracious as the young Human. It was wonderful, if exhausting, and Marrex was still amazed by how many times they'd had to replicate lubricant when Marrex's reserves ran out.

Sitting naked astride Marrex's thighs, Juniper continued brushing further down his chest, his expression one of concentration.

"You're unusually quiet," Marrex said.

Looking up from his grooming, Juniper just stared at the captain for a few moments before he lowered his eyes again. The brush caught a snarl and Marrex winced.

Juniper had been acting strange for three days now, ever since he'd called his family, but Marrex was hesitant to pry. It wasn't something Ghelyxians were comfortable doing... but then, Juniper was Human. They were a nosy, gregarious species, and judging by the pre-Contact Earth movies Juniper loved so much, maybe he was *supposed* to pry. He put his hand over Juniper's before he pulled a clump of fur out.

"What is it?" he asked quietly. "You can tell me."

The Human's brown eyes lifted to his again, and Marrex, as always, was captivated by the gilded patterns and fluctuating pupils that gave them so much expression. Marrex wished his own opaque black gaze could convey half of what went on in his mind.

But then, perhaps, Juniper would be scared off by the depths of his affection.

"I'm sorry. I have something to ask you... but, I've been putting it off because I don't know how you'll take it." As his dark eyebrows came together, Juniper licked his lips. He looked both nervous and guilty, and Marrex had to fight back some knee-jerk, panic-driven anger.

Marrex took a slow breath before replying. "I'm... listening."

Juniper searched his eyes. "You know how I said my father is sick?"

"I know." Heart sinking, Marrex took Juniper by the shoulders, giving them a gentle squeeze. He had a feeling he knew what was coming next. "You know I'm sorry he's not well."

"Thank you. And... well..." Juniper took a deep breath. "I want to go see him."

There was a lump in Marrex's throat so he didn't answer immediately. He'd been so naïve to think Juniper would stay.

"All right," he replied in a low voice.

"I know you're not supposed to go into Imperial space, but Terra Deux is barely on the edge... and if you can't take me yourself, I can take one of the shuttlepods. The *Stellerion* can drop me off near Peplum-3, and I'll go the rest of the way myself. But if you could take me the whole way, it would really mean a lot to me and—"

"When I said all right, I meant all right," Marrex replied curtly, the pain in his chest blooming. "I'll take you the whole way."

"What? You will?" Juniper looked astonished. "I thought you just meant, you know, 'all right' as in 'keep talking.'"

"Do you need anything? Money?" Marrex felt like he was shrivelling up inside, but it was for the best—he was just happy that he'd gotten to feel like a real person again, even for just a little while.

Again, Juniper's eyes went wide. "Yes... I could use some money."

"Take as much as you like. There are cases of jewels in the ship's holds. And I have almost a million credits I can transfer to you."

"You... do?"

"Take anything you like."

"Thank you," Juniper said, kissing him on the cheek. "You have *no* idea how much this means to me."

"You're welcome," Marrex replied, stroking down Juniper's smooth bare back. "You... mean a lot to me. I can't send you on your way without a token of my gratitude for the time we've spent together."

Juniper froze and pulled back, staring at Marrex. "You're not going to come get me?"

Marrex frowned, confused. "I assumed..."

"That I wasn't coming back? Of *course* I am, you ass," Juniper replied with a crooked grin. "Leave my poor monster all by his lonesome again? Not a chance." Juniper leaned in for another kiss, this time on Marrex's lips, and he put his arms around Marrex's neck.

The captain kissed Juniper back in a daze, his fur bristling down his back with excited relief. After a moment, he pushed Juniper back, scrutinizing him. The young man was pink cheeked and heavy lidded, a very familiar expression of lust— Marrex shook his head. "Are you certain?"

"Yes. I am certain, oh ye of little faith," Juniper replied with a laugh. "I'll show you just how certain I am," he continued, quickly unbuttoning the rest of Marrex's fly to pull out his soft cock.

Marrex snorted with amusement though he was still reeling from Juniper's assertion that he wasn't leaving him. "That's not going to work," he said, watching Juniper fondle him. He could probably get half-hard at *best*.

"No?"

"My body can't keep up with you," Marrex said, pulling Juniper's hands up so he could kiss them.

"Oh."

Juniper looked so disappointed that Marrex had to laugh, and then he sighed. "Believe me—I would indulge you if I could." Then he narrowed his eyes at Juniper, an idea coming to him. "Here," he said, "lie down this way. No, like this." Marrex helped Juniper stretch out across his lap with his head resting on his forearm, one leg dangling over the arm of the chair and the other hanging down between Marrex's knees. "Comfortable?"

"Comfortable enough," Juniper said, grinning. He had one hand around his hard shaft. "What are we doing?"

"We are giving my poor body a rest," Marrex replied, "and giving yours a workout that will guarantee your return to me."

"Oh?"

Marrex nodded. He shifted a bit in place to free his cock from under Juniper's back and pressed the underside to stimulate the glands there.

"What are you doing?" Juniper asked.

"You'll see." Marrex smiled and thumbed the hardening lump beneath his cockhead. He'd been thinking about this since reading up on Human anatomy and was curious to see what would happen. When he pushed up on the glands, some of the clear lubricating liquid swelled out of the ancillary slit, and he coated his forefinger with it. Now that his claws were blunt and short, he didn't fear hurting Juniper with them.

Juniper's full lips parted in astonishment when he obviously caught on to Marrex's intent, and his breathing sped up. Eagerly, he tilted his pelvis up and widened his knees further to give Marrex better access.

Marrex carefully slid his lube-covered finger into Juniper. Immediately, Juniper arched his back and gasped, releasing his cock, and Marrex chuckled. The stimulant in his lubricatory glands had a much milder effect on Ghelyxians... it was used to facilitate and enhance coitus, as well as improve chances of conception with females. Juniper's reaction was much more pronounced, to the point where Marrex sometimes worried for Juniper's heart.

In a few seconds, Marrex had easily located Juniper's prostate and began to run his finger in little circles over it, waiting for the lubricant to work its magic.

"Oh, that's good," Juniper said in a choked voice, his face red. He crushed his eyes closed and let out a wail and a grunt as the first climax took hold of him, sending an arc of ejaculate over Marrex's shoulder before painting his own stomach and chest with the rest. Juniper lay there panting and twitching as his sphincter pulsed around Marrex's knuckle, and Marrex let out a low, pleased growl. He'd barely begun stroking Juniper's sweet spot again before Juniper let out a ragged cry and came all over himself again.

"You like this?" Marrex said in a low voice.

"Yes... oh yes... fuh-uh-*fuck*!" Juniper yelled, pumping his hips as Marrex slowly fingered him into another orgasm.

"Good, because I can keep this up indefinitely."

"Oh god." There were already tears welling up in Juniper's eyes, and his body shuddered and jerked as he stared up at Marrex.

"A *very* long time," Marrex said, pleased with himself. He wondered how long it would take this time before Juniper begged him to stop. Hopefully, a long time. Then he would carry Juniper into their quarters, and he'd bathe him and tuck him into bed and cuddle him for the rest of the night while the *Stellerion* raced towards the Human's homeworld. And Marrex would lie there awake, trying to ignore the doubt burning in his belly.

CHAPTER 12
TERRA DEUX

J uniper climbed out of the transport ship, pushing the big fibrometal case on its hoverpad in front of him. Squinting in the harsh white light, he searched the small crowd for a familiar figure, but everyone looked the same in their protective suits from this distance. Slowly, he made his way over the cracked pavement, smiling hopefully at everyone he passed. However, the crowd began to disperse, and soon all travellers were accounted for, families and friends chatting happily as they left Juniper standing alone like an idiot on the tarmac.

Fucking Acacia and Willow, he thought angrily. They could have at least sent someone to come pick him up at the station if they couldn't be bothered to show up themselves. Annoyed, he pushed the case into the building and then queued up at the information counter to ask about getting a lift out to Port-Cartier. When it was finally his turn, the man at the counter just stared at the big metal case for a few seconds and shook his head. "Not until morning with that, I reckon," said the clerk. "Too big to fit in the hovercabs... you'll have to wait for the train."

Grinding his teeth, Juniper silently cursed out his sisters

again and keyed open one of the compartments on the side of the case. He pulled out a necklace of *delz* crystals, stones prized for their ability to block most types of radiation, and held them out to the man. The information clerk swallowed, staring at the crystals, then furtively looked from side to side and leaned forward.

"If you have another strand of those," the man said very quietly. "I'll give you my truck."

JUNIPER GROANED and rested his head on the steering wheel, frustrated by the delay. At this rate, he should have probably just waited for the train—the man's truck was an old-fashioned wheeled vehicle that required a nearly obsolete station that recharged the battery excruciatingly slow compared to modern vehicles. Juniper wondered if he'd get to Port-Cartier faster if he just walked.

"...per?" The communicator crystal in the necklace Marrex had given him let out a burst of loud static, then crackled softly, and again he heard S1N's voice. "Juniper? ...an you hear m..."

"S1N, I can barely hear you."

"You weren't...idding about the solar fla...s," said the AI. "What a crappy plan...t. Hang on. Compensating. Testing... check one, check two... sibilance...Juniper?"

"That's better," Juniper said. It was still crackly and faint, but at least S1N wasn't cutting in and out.

"I've been trying to reach you for three hours," S1N complained.

Frowning, Juniper cupped the large blue jewel of the communicator in his palm, his heart beating faster. "Why? What's wrong? Is Marrex all right? Where is he?"

"He's fine. He just wanted to see if you landed in one piece. I've let him know I've reached you. He'll be here in a second. I really didn't like the look of that old transport you took. Only fit for hauling livesto...n...my opinion."

"You're breaking up again. S1N? Can you hear me?" There was a long hissing crackle that went on for a few seconds.

"...ored enough to try fisting each oth..."

"*What?*" Juniper said, alarmed. "Hello?"

"Hello?"

It was just his own voice echoing back to him because of the interference, but he spoke slowly and carefully into the communicator in case S1N could hear him. "I landed fine. I'm now on my way home. I'm charging the truck I had to buy." Juniper looked at the battery gauge and saw that he still had about half an hour to go. He closed his eyes, trying to remember the last time he'd done the drive from Marseille to Port-Cartier. Juniper figured he could make it on a partial charge.

"I'll try boosting the signal when I get home," he said, hoping S1N was listening. "Tell Marrex not to worry about me, ok?"

Fuck it. He hit the release, then pressed his thumb to the screen on the console to pay his credits.

THE HOUSE LOOKED MUCH as it had the day he left. It was a low, wide building covered in rad shielding done up to resemble marble—with eight bedrooms within, it was a huge mansion in this part of the world. As he got closer, however, he noticed many of the tiles were cracked and needed replacing, and every nook and overhang was covered in what was known locally as *crud*—a yellowish mixture of dirt and vellus spores that baked hard in the burning sunshine. It got on everything and was a pain in the ass to scrape off. Judging by the look of the siding, no one had taken a chisel to it in years.

Having no key, he knocked on the door, waited, and banged again when no one answered. Annoyed, he tried the handle and saw that it was unlocked so he let himself into the vestibule, dragging the fibrometal case behind him.

"Hello?" he called, folding back the sealant tabs on his face mask. The suit was a cheap tourist one, much patched and smelling of the disinfectant they used to clean it, but he'd figured it wasn't worth it to buy a new one since he wouldn't be there very long. Juniper dropped the mask and gloves into a bin by the door and unzipped the rest of the suit, sighing with relief as he peeled it off himself. He was sweaty, tired, and hungry... and pissed off.

Pushing open the interior door, he came face to face with a very startled Acacia.

"Juniper! You're here..." she said.

"Where were you?" he said as he stepped forward.

"Whoa whoa whoa, mister," Acacia said, holding her hands up. "You're tracking in dirt. Leave the suit in there."

Scowling, Juniper stepped back and finished undressing, kicking off his boots. "Why the hell didn't you come pick me up?"

"I must have gotten the date wrong," Acacia replied, handing a broom to Juniper.

"What? *Really*? I had to buy a truck to get here." He angrily swept up the tiny pile of dirt, and as he did so, he noticed that the flooring had been replaced with real wood, quite a luxury on Terra Deux. Then he lifted his head and looked around. When he'd left seventeen years ago, the rooms had been almost bare. Now, they were full of what looked like expensive furniture and artwork. Even Acacia's dress looked pricey.

Obviously noticing Juniper's scrutiny, Acacia frowned and flapped her hand at their surroundings. "There was a class action against the company after the colony ship was lost... and we got some money in the settlement," Acacia explained. "But it's all gone now," she was quick to add. "We've started selling things off—"

"Juniper!" Willow walked into the room, her arms held out. "You're here!"

He accepted the hug, awkward as it was, then smiled. "I am." *No thanks to you.*

"Where are your bags?" Willow asked, looking behind him.

"Uh... I just have this case." He went back to the vestibule and pulled the case through the door.

His sisters shared a look, and then Acacia clasped her hands in front of her, smiling though it didn't reach her eyes. "That's... big. How long were you planning on staying?"

"Not long. I need to get back to my... ah, friend," Juniper replied, feeling conspicuous. "I brought some money and things to help out with Dad."

"Oh?" Willow's eyes were on the case. "What kind of things?"

Juniper keyed in his code and opened a few compartments. "Um, *delz* crystals. Some nanoscrubbers. A bunch of fibrotitanium calipers and driveshafts. Oh, and two brand-new diamond drill heads..."

"Junk?" Acacia's voice was cold.

"Not junk... you'll still able to get a hell of a lot for this stuff."

"Yes, but we still have to *sell* it," Willow said wearily, pinching the bridge of her nose. "Oh, Juniper, I thought you were going to bring *credits*."

Juniper stared at her. The rings she wore would easily fetch a few thousand credits each. Something wasn't right here. He decided not to mention the million credits Marrex had given him—not yet.

"Where's Dad?"

"He's sleeping at the moment," Acacia replied. "You can see him later." She held out her hand.

"What?" Juniper asked, looking at her empty palm.

"The *delz* crystals?" Acacia replied, arching one brow.

"I'll take care of selling everything," he said, pushing the compartments closed. "It's not a problem."

"Fine," Acacia replied. "That'll have to do."

"We were just about to sit down for some supper..." Willow said, looking over at Acacia. "I guess you can join us."

"Why, thank you for your *enormous* generosity," Juniper said. "Why are the two of you being so awful? I would have thought you'd be glad to see me."

"Sorry, Juniper," Acacia said with a sigh. "We *are* glad to see you. It's just... it's been difficult."

Willow clasped Juniper's arm and looked up at him, her blue eyes wide. "Acacia's husband passed last year... and with the storms and solar flares getting worse... it's been hard to keep up with repairs without his help and"—she looked up at the ceiling, blowing a little air out of pursed lips—"God only knows if Dad is ever going to get better... oh, and the market prices lately, Juny... it's just awful."

Juniper nodded sympathetically. He knew how challenging life in Port-Cartier could be—maybe he *was* overreacting. "I'm sorry, I'm just cranky from travelling," he replied, patting her hand. "Why don't I go put this in my room and freshen up, and then I'll join you for supper?"

"I'll get the soup warmed," Acacia said, walking away.

Juniper touched the lift button on the hoverpad and the case rose into the air. He took a few steps toward his old room.

"You're staying in the guest room, Juny."

"What? Why? What's wrong with my old room?"

"It's Peggy's now," Willow said. "Acacia's daughter?"

"Oh. Well... what happened to my stuff?" Juniper had been looking forward to wearing some of his old clothes.

"It's gone. I'm sorry, sweetie."

"Gone?"

"You've been *dead* for seventeen years."

"You didn't keep *anything*?" he said, a sour taste in his

mouth.

Willow winced and shook her head.

Juniper just stared at her for a moment, then turned quickly away so she wouldn't see his tears, and dragged the case behind him to the back of the house.

"S1N? VAL? DO YOU READ ME?" Juniper said, sitting on the edge of the guest bed. He frowned at the comm-crystal in his palm. "Anyone?" When there was no reply after several seconds, he set the communicator to ping the *Stellerion* every thirty seconds while he went to wash his face and hands in the small bathroom.

Finding the bathroom without water, Juniper closed his eyes and stood with his fists balled, trying to calm himself down before reaching for the nozzle of the particle wash. He cleaned himself off as best as he could in the stinging beam, purposefully taking his time—it was petty to retaliate by wasting electricity, but he couldn't help himself. Red-eyed and pale, he glared at his reflection in the mirror, trying to untangle the mess of his hair, when the blue jewel around his neck beeped then let out a loud crackle.

"Juniper?"

"S1N... am I glad to hear your voice. Is Marrex there? Can I talk to him?"

"Sorry, we've docked, and the captain is taking care of a little business. I'd patch you through but these darkmarket traders are so paranoid. Captain Marrex'll be back by the end of this cycle—that's three hours from now, your time."

"Oh. Ok."

"What's wrong, kiddo? You sound down."

"I don't know what I was expecting," Juniper said as he walked back to the small guest room. He sighed, shaking his head. "But it wasn't this."

"They didn't have a Welcome Home, Juniper! banner up?" S1N asked.

Juniper let out a bitter little laugh. "No. I never really got along with my sisters when I was a kid, but that was sibling rivalry stuff, you know? But I just assumed they'd give a shit if I was dead." He stared at the pile of bedding on the bare mattress. "They didn't even make up a bed for me... And they threw out everything I owned. Not a keepsake left. Nothing."

"I'm sorry, Juniper. That's terrible," VAL said.

"Downright shitty," S1N added.

"Thanks, guys," Juniper said, his eyes burning. "God... why did I come?"

"To see your father. How is he?" asked VAL.

"I haven't even seen him yet—" Juniper lifted his head, listening hard. He heard Willow's voice again and she sounded annoyed. "I have to go. I'll call again in three hours."

"I'll be here," S1N replied.

Juniper touched his thumb to the side of the comm-crystal but didn't press down. "Hey... how is he?" he asked softly.

There was no response for a few seconds, and he thought he had accidentally closed the connection. Then S1N spoke up. "He's fine. He'll be fine. Just come home to us, ok?"

"Ok."

JUNIPER STARED into his bowl of pea soup, spooning up mouthfuls mechanically while his sisters basically ignored him. They were busy fussing over Peggy's upcoming debutante ball and giving her all sorts of nonsensical and frankly appalling advice on how to be more ladylike. He snorted to himself, shaking his head. Poor Peggy seemed like a sweet kid, but it was obvious that she was far more interested in joining the Port-Cartier razerball squad than she was in joining polite society. Juniper had enjoyed his own "deb ball," as they were known colloquially, but that was only because of numerous trips to the broom closet to trade hip flasks and blow jobs with the other deb boys. He smiled to himself, remembering the look on Mr. Rayned's face when he'd found Juniper with his pants down around his ankles, waiting for his friend Simon to join him. Juniper had arched an eyebrow at him and said, "Are you in or out?" to which Mr. Rayned had given a stuttering reply, declining, before shutting the closet door again.

"What's funny?" said Willow.

Juniper looked up, startled. "Oh... nothing. Just remembering stuff."

"So, Juniper, you're working on a ship now?" Acacia asked, sprinkling more salt into her soup.

"I am."

"What is it you do?"

"Odd jobs, mostly. The ship's huge, but there's only the captain and me to keep her running."

"So... you're a handyman?" Acacia said slowly, her brows raised in disbelief.

Juniper chuckled and gave a shrug. "I guess so." He thought he heard the faint sound of a bell.

"Why is there no crew?" Peggy asked, visibly relieved that she was no longer the topic of conversation.

"Marrex just prefers it that way. He's very private," Juniper replied.

"Marrex? He's this 'friend' you mentioned? The captain?" Willow asked.

"Yeah." He looked back down to his soup.

"You're blushing!" Willow said, grinning. "Are you two more than friends?"

"I am *not* blushing," Juniper said, scowling. Then he sighed and chuckled again. "And yes, you could say that."

"Oh my," Acacia replied archly. "You've bagged yourself a captain then, have you?"

"What does he look like? Is he handsome?" asked Peggy.

"*I* think he is," Juniper said, glancing over at his niece. "But you probably wouldn't."

"Why not?"

"Well... he's"—Juniper cleared his throat, stirring what was left of his soup—"Ghelyxian."

For a moment, it was so silent Juniper could hear his pulse in his ears.

Then Willow shook her head. "Oh, Juny..." she said in disgust.

"What?" Juniper replied, annoyed.

"You always did make poor choices," Acacia said, shaking her head.

"I don't understand," Peggy said quietly. "What's wrong with Ghelyxians?"

"Absolutely *nothing*," Juniper replied. The bell rang again faintly, and he frowned, wondering what it was.

"They're hideous, Peggy," Willow said. "Big and furry and bright-red like the Devil. Horned too. And they are completely insufferable with all their laws and regulations. It's because of *them* that Terra Deux doesn't qualify for full aid during the winter."

"Oh," said Peggy, staring round-eyed at Juniper.

"Marrex doesn't have anything to do with that," Juniper retorted. "And he's not hideous."

"Peggy, sweetheart," Acacia said. "Your uncle has always had a strange fascination with aliens. He thinks it's perfectly acceptable to... dally with them." From her tone, it was obvious that any similar behaviour by her daughter would not be tolerated.

"No one says 'aliens' anymore... it's derogatory," Juniper muttered.

"I don't care," Acacia replied, curling her lip. "It's unnatural."

"Juny, be *smart* and stop thinking only about yourself," Willow said. "How is it going to look for your family if you're off doing god knows what with an ali—uh, offworlder? Think of your niece! Can you imagine what she'll go through if it becomes known that her uncle is... *associating* with something like that?"

Juniper ground his teeth together and shook his head, breathing slowly through his nose.

You wish *you were lucky enough to have someone like Marrex associate with* you...

"It's my life," he said in a low voice. The bell gave another plaintive jingle, and Juniper turned towards the sound—it was coming from inside the house. "What *is* that ringing?"

"It's nothing," Acacia said. "He'll stop in a bit."

"*He?*" Juniper said in alarm. "Is that *Dad*?"

"It's nothing," repeated his sister. "We'll go check on him after we eat."

Standing, Juniper wiped his mouth. "Let me see him. Now."

"Really, Juny... don't be so dramatic!" Willow said, a grimace on her face. "He's in his room, the same one he always had. But really, he just rings the bell to get attention..."

Feeling sick to his stomach, Juniper jogged down the hall to the other end of the house and threw open the door to his father's room. Immediately, he recoiled, covering his mouth and nose with his sleeve, the smell of urine and sickness heavy in the air. The room beyond was darkened, but he could make out a pale figure sprawled atop a mattress on the floor. His eyes quickly adjusted, and taking a step into the room, he saw that his father was tied to the mattress by one wrist and the opposite ankle. The little golden bell his father held gave another faint jingle as he shifted, his eyes wide and staring.

"Oh my god," he whispered hoarsely. "Dad?"

"It looks sort of bad, but we had to tie him up or he'd go wandering outside," Willow said quietly from behind him.

Juniper saw the crotch of his father's pyjamas was dark, and he guessed he'd wet himself. "Was he ringing the bell because he had to go to the bathroom?"

"I don't know and neither does he. Has to pee, doesn't have to pee—he rings it all the time. Drives us crazy with it."

"Drives *you* crazy? How do you think *he* feels?"

"I wish I knew!" Willow said, exasperated. "He hasn't spoken a word since '28."

"This is *wrong*."

"If we could afford a full-time nurse, we'd get one," Acacia said, stepping into the room. She wrinkled her nose at the smell and shook her head, gazing down at the man on the mattress. "We just don't have that kind of money. Keep your criticisms to yourself... you weren't here."

"You've got him locked up like an animal in here," Juniper said, completely revolted by the neglect. "Dad? Dad, it's me." He went down on his knees next to the mattress, trying not to breathe through his nose. "It's Juniper."

There was no recognition in his father's eyes—he just stared blankly at Juniper for a few seconds, and then his gaze wandered over to the wall. Juniper cleared his throat, trying to keep the tears from falling, and reached for his father's hand. It was cold and thin in his grasp, the nails far too long. "Don't worry, Dad. I'll clean you up." Lifting his head, he glared at his sisters who had the sense to look ashamed of themselves. "Acacia, open those curtains. Peggy, go run a bath and—"

"A *bath*? We can't afford that much water!" Willow exclaimed.

"I can," Juniper said. "I have the credits. Just go run that bath."

"Yes, Uncle Juniper."

"And one of you call the hospital. He needs a doctor."

"He's *seen* a doct—" Willow started.

"*Now*," Juniper barked. To his surprise, Willow jumped to

obey.

Acacia slowly tied the curtain back, letting in the bright sun, and Juniper clenched his jaw as the light revealed the mottled bruising and abrasions around his father's wrist and ankle.

"My god. You're monsters," Juniper said faintly.

"*You weren't here*," Acacia repeated, her words terse. "You can't know what we've been through. It's just been too much, Juniper. I know it looks bad, but you have to understand..."

"Understand what? This is abuse."

"Don't *exaggerate*. I would have put him in a home, Juniper. But we just don't have money for that. Peggy needed to go to school... Arthur... my husband... his funeral... we just..." Acacia's voice broke.

Juniper glanced up, startled to see Acacia on the verge of tears. He'd never seen Acacia cry, not even the day their father had confessed to losing everything.

She wiped her nose, looking away from him. "I took good care of him, Juniper. I swear. When we got that settlement, it was a godsend. We had a nurse here to look after Dad. But it could only last for so long... you have *no* idea of the sacrifices we've made. After a while, you just have to start making choices..."

"So you chose to keep Dad locked in his room, pissing himself in the dark?" Juniper was so disgusted he could barely think straight.

"He gets cleaned regularly, I promise. It's not like we leave him here like this for days. But it's just... he has no idea what's happening. He doesn't care. There's nothing left of Dad..."

"He's just a burden then? Not a priority? You're *sick* and you're *selfish*."

"You weren't *here*," Acacia repeated weakly.

"Just fuck off and go away," Juniper muttered. He turned back to his father and gently pried the bell out of his grasp. "It's ok, Dad. I'm here..."

CHAPTER 13
STIMULATION AND INTERFERENCE

The doctor looked over the chart on his tablet and clicked his tongue quietly against his teeth a few times before answering. "Well... he's healthy enough," he said, glancing up at Juniper. "His wrist and ankle can be easily treated with some antibiotic cream, so can his bed sores, and I'll give you a different cream for his rash. But, he's been fed adequately and despite the muscle atrophy, he's in good shape."

Acacia scoffed. "See?"

"*But*," the doctor continued with a stern look for Acacia, "he needs far more mental stimulation than what he's been getting."

"So what's wrong with him? Why is he like this?" Juniper asked. His father was lying on his back on the hospital bed with wires attached to him all over, his expression blank.

"I don't really have an answer for you. When his son was lost, he suffered severe emotional and psychological trauma that left him like... this. There's nothing physically wrong with him."

"It's all in his head, you mean?" Juniper frowned.

"*Yes*," the doctor replied hesitantly, "though it's not as simple as that."

"But, I'm his son, and I'm not dead—shouldn't that have snapped him out of it when he saw me?"

The doctor blinked rapidly a few times, looked down at the tablet in his hand, then back up at Juniper. "Ah... I'm sorry? I don't understand. It says here his son was lost in 427, age twenty-two. You look..." He gestured at Juniper in confusion.

"Twenty-two. Yeah, I know," Juniper said. "I guess I'm technically almost forty." He laughed at the look on the doctor's face. "The reports of my death were greatly exaggerated," he said, using the famous Twain misquote. "I was actually in stasis for the last seventeen years."

"That's incredible," the doctor said, his eyes wide. "I've never met anyone who's been in stasis for so long. Did you have any side effects? How's your general health?"

"Um. Not that I've noticed, and I guess my health is ok?" Juniper thought about the brief scans he'd done on himself aboard the *Stellerion*. Had they been enough? The equipment was ancient... what if they didn't pick up something that was wrong with him? "I'm not actually sure."

"Would you allow me to run a few tests? I'd like to see—"

The comm-crystal hanging from Juniper's neck gave a loud squawk and then hissed for a few seconds. "Juniper?"

Juniper was incredibly relieved to hear the sound of Marrex's voice, but he had things to sort out first. He turned his back to the others and lifted the crystal closer to his mouth. "Marrex, I'm here but I can't talk right now. Bad timing. I'll call you back as soon as I can."

"...right?" There was another hiss and a crackle, then nothing at all.

"Marrex?" Juniper said, but the comm was silent. He hoped the captain had heard what he'd said. Sighing, he turned back to the doctor.

"Fine, you can run any test you want on me, but in return, you're going to waive your fee for today," he said.

"Yes, of course. That's fine," said the doctor. Though the man's face was young, his hair was silver, and the few lines at the corners of his eyes betrayed the truth of his age. He scrutinized Juniper for a few moments, his blue eyes narrowed, and Juniper thought he was handsome in a bland sort of way.

"But, what's your advice for treating my father?" Juniper asked.

"Stimulus... it doesn't have to be much—read to him, let him watch vids. I'm going suggest some injections of a stimulant to see if his catatonia responds."

"Thank you," Juniper replied.

"As long as you pay for the injections," Acacia said.

Juniper stared at her, irritated at her pettiness even after he'd saved them a few thousand credits by volunteering to guinea pig. After a moment, Acacia looked away, her lips pressed together, and didn't say another word.

"...CAN'T talk right n...w ...ad timing. I'll call you back as s...n as I can" came Juniper's reply before a blast of deafening static filled the bridge.

Wincing, Marrex asked, "Are you all right?" but the console had already fallen silent, the connection lost or closed.

Marrex stared at the blinking lights, trying not to let his disappointment and dread show, but it was obvious he was doing a poor job because when S1N tilted his head to look up at Marrex his eyes were wide with uncharacteristic sympathy.

"I'm sure he'll call soon," the AI said, the tip of his tail flicking. "He probably had a very good reason to end the call."

"Perhaps," Marrex grumbled, standing. "I'll be in my quarters. Let me know immediately when he calls."

"Sure thing, boss," S1N replied.

"Immediately," VAL added, his face shimmering like a pale opal.

Marrex trudged slowly down the hall to his room. Juniper was among his own kin and kind again... it was probably for the best. He punched the button to open the door and stepped into his darkened quarters. Eyes closed, he breathed in deep, smelling the air. There was Juniper... his warm, smooth skin, the shampoo he used in his hair, the subtle salt of the helpless tears he cried during their mating, the slight acrid smell of his seed... Heaving a long sigh, Marrex sank down onto the mattress, his shoulders hunched forward and face in his hands. The ache in his chest like nothing he'd ever felt before.

"Juniper," he whispered. "Where are you?"

WITH PEGGY'S HELP, Juniper cleaned out his father's room and set up the hospital bed he'd rented. It had high sides with special openings where he could pass a soft restraint across his father's middle, tied beneath the bed where his father couldn't reach. The sheets were new and crisp and so were the pajamas they'd purchased on the way home. Slowly, Juniper wheeled his father to his bed, and then carefully lifted him onto it. He smiled as he tucked him in.

"There you go, Dad. Isn't this better?"

His father's eyes wandered in their sockets, never settling on one thing for more than an instant, and his hand was limp when Juniper squeezed it. His face contorted for an instant, as if in pain, but the doctor had told him it was just part of his catatonia and didn't mean he was in any discomfort. However, Juniper found it hard to look at. "I'll be right back with some food. I just need to make a quick call first."

Juniper escaped to the guest room and shut the door,

rubbing his face. He was thoroughly exhausted and emotionally drained, and he had no idea how long he'd been awake—Terran days were longer than the Imperial Standard they kept aboard the *Stellerion*, and he was suffering from space-lag. Now that he had five minutes to himself, all he wanted to do was hear Marrex's voice and talk about absolutely nothing before he had to go make food for his dad.

Lying back on his bed, Juniper lifted the blue comm-crystal. "Marrex? Come in?"

For a few seconds, there was nothing but a quiet hum layered over the hiss of static, then, "Juniper! How are you?"

"Hi, VAL, I'm ok. Can I please talk to Marrex?"

"Uh. Hm. It looks like he's asleep… it's very late here. Shall I go wake him?"

"*Crap*…" Juniper pinched the bridge of his nose, grimacing. He felt so crummy and miserable that he was nearly in tears.

"Juniper?"

"I've only got a few minutes to talk—it's not worth waking him up. Can you just give him a message when he gets up?"

"Of course, Juniper." VAL's voice was faint and crackly over the connection.

"Tell him I'll call the next time I have a few minutes. Oh… and tell him I miss him? I'm sure he'd like to hear that. It's just been a mess here… I don't even know where to start."

There was a loud crackle, and the hiss of white noise got louder. Juniper tapped on the crystal to adjust the squelch.

"VAL? Did you hear me?"

A stream of garbled noises came from the crystal and then silence. Juniper cursed to himself, trying to restore the connection.

The door banged open, and Willow poked her head into the room. "*There* you are, Juny. I've been looking all over. If you want to use the stove, now's your chance. Oh… and while you're in the kitchen, could you take a look at the garburator, please? It started to do this thing"—Willow made a harsh growling sound while twirling one finger slowly in the air—"and I remember you fixed it that one time."

Taking a deep breath, Juniper sat up, nodding wearily. "Sure. Whatever. I'll take a look."

MARREX SNORTED and tossed his head, his fists balled so hard that his blunt claws pressed painfully into his palms, cutting his flesh.

"Why...didn't...you...wake...me?" he said very slowly, his voice a low growl.

VAL's holoprojection was nearly transparent, his eyes huge in his tiny face. "I'm sorry, sir. Juniper said not to."

"I said *immediately*. I didn't say 'maybe later.' I didn't say 'whenever you get around to it.' I said to let me know immediately when he called." Marrex was so furious he could barely see. Had the AI a neck, he would have wrapped his hands around it.

"Captain," S1N said, floating up to face him. "Juniper said he had only a few minutes to talk. You *know* how hard it is to wake you up sometimes... you sleep like a corpse. I'm sure you would have missed each other."

Marrex bared his teeth, flaring his nostrils as he glared at the AI.

"Th-that's not to say we shouldn't have tried waking you," S1N continued, retreating a few steps. "It won't happen again."

"It won't, sir," agreed VAL. "And he left you a message."

"He did? What is it?"

"I... I'm afraid I don't know," VAL replied nervously. "There was too much interference... but"—VAL's face shrunk even further as Marrex let out a deep growl, stepping forward—"I'm certain he had something nice to say."

Marrex threw back his head, roaring out of frustration, and S1N leapt back, his fur standing on end. VAL just disappeared completely.

"I'm... going to try him now," S1N said quickly. "Stand by, Captain."

JUNIPER WIGGLED the wrench back and forth, trying to free the bottommost nut. Finally, after struggling with it for a few minutes, it turned. He sat up, wiping his forehead, and looked over at Peggy who'd just come into the kitchen.

"Everything ok?" he asked.

"Grandpa ate almost everything, and then I read a little to him," she said, setting down the tray with dirty dishes. "He fell asleep almost right away. I think the trip to the hospital tired him out."

"Probably," Juniper replied. "When was the last time he was out of that room?"

"I can't remember," Peggy said. She cleared her throat and looked down, her blonde brows drawn together. "Uncle Juniper... I should have done something and I'm sorry."

Juniper smiled at Peggy. "You're just a kid... you're what? Fifteen?"

"That's no excuse. I could have read to him every day after school. I could have gotten a job on the weekends... maybe at the market. You know, to help out a bit."

"Well, you're doing something now," Juniper said, lying down to tackle the next rusted nut. "That's what counts. And I appreciate it."

The comm-crystal let out a burst of static. "Juniper?"

"There you are!" he said, sitting back up. He misjudged the distance to the counter in his excitement and cracked his forehead on the rim of it. "Ow, *fuck*."

125

"Juniper? What happened?" Marrex's voice was hoarse and words abrupt as though he were beside himself with worry.

"Nothing. I just hit my head on the counter. I'm doing some repairs. How did you sleep?"

"Those idiots were supposed to wake me," Marrex growled. The connection hissed and crackled, eradicating the next words.

"I can barely hear you," Juniper said.

"...is better?"

"There's only so much you can do on your end," he said quickly. "Listen, first thing tomorrow morning, I'm going to go clean the crud off the relays on the roof. I don't think anyone's done that in a long time, and it'll definitely help."

"...niper?"

Juniper groaned in frustration. "Marrex?" He shook the blue jewel even though he knew that wouldn't make a difference. The comm-crystal crackled again, and the line went silent.

"Shit."

"Juniper, are you still there?" Marrex sounded far away, like he was at the bottom of a well, but his voice was clear.

"I am. I just said I'll try to improve the connection on my end tomorrow after I get some sleep."

"All right." Marrex was silent for a few seconds. "How... are you?"

"I'm ok. Just dead tired," Juniper said, then yawned as though proving his point. "I have a bunch of things to take care of here, but when I'm done... Marrex, would it be ok if I brought my father aboard the *Stellerion*?"

The connection hissed and snapped, obscuring any reply. Juniper heard a noise to his right and glanced over. Acacia was staring at him with an odd expression on her thin face, and he scowled at her. "What?"

"What what?" Marrex replied, his voice tinny.

"Sorry, I was talking to my sister." He looked down at the

crystal in his hand. "Listen, I have to go. We'll talk later." Juniper felt his sister's eyes on him and hunched his shoulders, feeling uncomfortable under her scrutiny. "I... uh... miss you," he said quietly and looked back up as his sister scoffed and walked away. "Marrex?" He tapped and shook the crystal some more, but it was obvious that the connection was lost. Juniper let out a long sigh of defeat and sagged back against the counter, pressing his palms against his eyelids.

"You'll be back home soon."

Home... Juniper lifted his head, having forgotten about his niece. He sighed again and nodded. "I know. I'm just"—he rubbed his forehead, blinking to dry his weary tears—"tired."

Peggy sat down cross-legged on the floor in front of him, her forehead wrinkled in sympathy. For the first time, Juniper noticed that she had the same eyes as him, and for some reason that endeared her to him even more. He gave her a sad smile. "I'll be all right."

"Tell me about your captain," Peggy said, resting her cheek on her hand. "What's he like?"

Juniper thought for a moment, then chuckled. "Well, he's bossy, but at the same time, he's seriously lacking in self-confidence, so he takes everything as an insult and blows his top easily. And he can be cold and distant, but I think that's because he's Ghelyxian. Oh, and he snores something awful."

Peggy made a face. "He sounds wonderful."

Laughing, Juniper held out his hand. "Pass me the pliers." He took them from Peggy and resumed his work on the broken garburator. "I don't know him all that well, to be honest. He was alone for such a long time. Getting him to talk sometimes feels like chipping away at a boulder... but when he *does* relax, he's just really... great. He can be funny, sometimes without meaning to be, and he's smart. Did I mention he was a prince?" He looked over at Peggy and she shook her head. "He can dance and speak a bunch of languages, and he's got these manners that just... I don't know." Juniper let out another laugh. "I like how proper he can be. And he's attentive and really concerned about making me happy, like I'm someone really special..." He swallowed, frowning through the tears that had sprung up in his eyes, and the motor assembly swam in his vision.

"It sounds like you love him very much," Peggy said quietly.

Juniper snorted, shaking his head. "Love? I don't know..." he replied. "I *like* him. I don't know if I'd call that love." He smirked self-consciously and reached out to gently swat at his niece's knee. "You're fifteen... what do you know about love? Hm?" However, he sobered when he saw the look on her face.

"What is it?"

"Promise not to tell my mother?" she said in a low voice.

Juniper mimed locking his lips. "Of course."

"I've been secretly seeing a boy from my class."

"Oh?" Juniper grinned.

"And... he's Cebari," she whispered.

Juniper blinked at her. The Cebari were a hyperintelligent insectoid species native to Terra Deux—seemed it wasn't only Juniper's eyes she inherited.

"Oh my," he said, amused.

Peggy grinned back at him.

CHAPTER 14
SABOTAGE

After the rooftop relays had been scraped clean, communication was vastly improved, but Juniper was kept so busy with repairs and hospital tests and getting his father's affairs in order that there was barely time to talk to Marrex. For some reason, every time he settled down to call the captain, one of his sisters would demand he fix yet another thing or head to the market to trade the items he brought for credits they could use. As such, the conversations he managed to have with Marrex were always too short and he could tell from the Ghelyxian's curt responses that it wasn't sitting well with him.

Frustrated by the lack of change in his father's condition, his sisters' constant demands, and by Marrex's growing diffidence, Juniper's fuse was getting shorter by the day. It had been two weeks, and it would be at least one more before he could return to the *Stellerion*. Scowling to himself as he stood under the stinging particle shower, Juniper thought about what needed to be accomplished before he could leave. Part of him knew it was stupid... why was he bothering with these repairs? Why should he care? It's not as if the relationship with his sisters had improved.

I should just leave them to fix everything, he thought as he turned off the shower. However, he knew he would feel guilty if he just left them in the lurch. At least this way, he could part ways with them with a clear conscience. He quickly brushed the fine dust off his skin and went back to his room, ready to start the day. Juniper pushed open the door to his room and froze.

Willow stood next to the fibrometal case, and from the guilty look on her face, Juniper guessed she'd been trying to open the compartments.

"What are you doing?" he asked, glaring at her.

Wincing, his sister gestured helplessly towards the case. "I was going to the market. I just thought…"

"It's biolocked. And why go to the market? The cellar stores are full, what more do you need?"

"I thought… maybe some wine?"

"If you want wine, why don't you sell those rings?" he said, annoyed at her intrusion.

"You're right," Willow replied, looking down at her hands. She sighed. "I'll do that. Sorry, Juny." She lifted her eyes to his, her smile timid. "Would you like some? I'll get a few bottles of something we can all enjoy together. Do you still like those sweet Alsatian reds?"

Willow's offer seemed genuine, and he was touched she remembered his favourite wine—out of his sisters, he'd always liked Willow more, so Juniper sighed, relenting. "Fine… here." He popped open one of the smaller compartments and placed a small *delz* crystal in her palm. "Save your rings for when I'm gone," he said. "Go get some wine. And… look to see if they have something called *leb*." The stimulating drink would help him get through the rest of the long Terran days.

As Juniper watched his sister go, he reached for the comm-crystal he'd hung on the hook next to his bed, and put it back around his neck.

MARREX LAY on his side in the grass, his eyes closed. He breathed slowly in through his nose and then out his mouth, trying to quiet his heart.

Juniper wasn't coming back.

The pain was more than he could bear.

JUNIPER COUGHED, covering his mouth, revolted by the stench of decay that hung like a green cloud all around him. Huge, mutated plants rose up to each side of the path, their sickly leaves covered in black slime. Stepping forward, he cried out in pain. The path was made of broken glass, and his feet were bare. He knew it was a dream... but that didn't stop things from hurting like hell.

There was a rustle in the bushes to his left, and a swarm of flies took to the air as a small form emerged. Juniper saw it was the tiny Ghelyxian, and he smiled with relief, but when it approached, it growled, showing its yellow fangs. The poor thing looked like it had been severely beaten—its fur was matted and dark with blood, and one of its eyes was swollen shut.

"Hey," Juniper said softly, crouching down despite the shards of glass piercing the soles of his feet. "What happened?"

The Ghelyxian recoiled from him, hissing and growling, and Juniper slowly extended his hand, trying to soothe the little beast.

"Hey, it's ok," he murmured, but when he finally touched it, it sank its teeth into his finger. "*Fuck!*" Juniper shouted and fell, landing on his backside in the broken glass. Howling with pain, he jumped to his feet, then crashed headlong into an oozing pile of vegetation. By the time he'd freed himself, he was covered head to toe in blood and stinking slime. Juniper gagged and retched, crawling towards the clearing where he found the Ghelyxian manikin lying on its side, its eyes closed. It let out a plaintive little mewl, and Juniper was about to ask it again what happened when he heard a low, pain-filled groan echo the little Ghelyxian's cry.

Startled, Juniper looked around. "Hello?" In all the dozens of times he'd had the garden dream, there had never been anyone else with him except the small living statue.

Another moan came from behind him, and Juniper stood, finding himself at the edge of a square pit. At the bottom lay a big shape that shuddered and groaned again. "Who's there?"

The moon came out from behind the clouds, illuminating the pit's occupant, and Juniper pressed the back of his hand to his mouth. The Ghelyxian in the pit was misshapen and twisted, its deformed muscles bulging through random patches in its shaggy fur, sharp teeth turned to yellow tusks that split its lips and skewed its mouth. There were too many horns sprouting from its head, the sharp ends turning back on themselves to dig into its flesh. Slowly, the Ghelyxian's eyes opened, and Juniper was horrified.

"Marrex?"

Marrex let out another long moan, and Juniper leaned forward to get a better look. He thought he was going to be sick—Marrex was covered in weeping sores and strange growths.

"Oh god... what happened to you?" he whispered.

The little Ghelyxian, now bright-red and whole, stood on the opposite side of the pit, pointing an accusatory finger at Juniper.

"What? What did *I* do?"

The little creature jabbed his finger again, his lip curled in a sneer.

"Hey, it's not my fault I haven't been able to reach him. I've tried, trust me! Even the house comm is on the fritz—probably solar flares. I'm sure it'll clear up soon... and it's not like he's tried to reach me either. Besides... it's only been two days."

The manikin shook his head, crossing its tiny arms.

"Ok, *three* days. I've been busy."

The little Ghelyxian shook his head again.

Juniper frowned. The creature was right... three Terran days was the equivalent to approximately four aboard the *Stellerion*. He rubbed his face, wishing he could wake up. This was just his subconscious guilt-tripping him for not trying harder to reach Marrex. But it really wasn't his fault...

Whose fault is it then? The strange thought came out of nowhere, and he lifted his head, startled. The wind blew softly, bringing with it a quiet tinkling, like a glass wind chime. Juniper scanned the surrounding foliage for the source and saw a monstrous tree at the far end of the clearing, its long drooping branches filled with blue crystals. Head tilted, Juniper approached, both curious and strangely tense. The tree was misshapen like everything else in the corrupted garden. Its base was bulbous and covered in sickly, oozing patches, and the crystals swayed in the wind, their chiming music more rhythmic than seemed natural... Juniper squinted, trying to recall where he'd seen something like that before, the memory like a word on the tip of his tongue.

The crystals were blue...

The blue crystals were swaying back and forth...

The swaying blue crystals were in the branches of a tree...

Juniper shook his head, trying to concentrate.

Swaying blue crystals in the long drooping branches of a *willow* tree.

JUNIPER'S EYES SNAPPED OPEN, and he sat up, his heart pounding. The alarm was chiming, taking over from his dream, and he snapped his fingers to stop it. Quickly, he opened the back of the comm-crystal around his neck and immediately saw the relay chip was missing.

Of course, he thought, his mouth dry. He was sure if he looked into the house communicator, he'd find it was also missing some necessary component. No wonder he couldn't connect to the *Stellerion*.

Furious, Juniper swung his legs over the side of the bed and grabbed his pants in one motion, throwing them on in a haste.

I'm stupid. He'd been so distracted by Willow trying to open the big case that he had only faintly registered the blue comm-crystal swaying on its hook. He could see it now in his memory, the motion slight out of the corner of his eye. *Stupid, stupid, stupid.*

Juniper burst into the dining room where his sisters and niece were just sitting down to breakfast, and he wrenched Willow's chair back so he could lean over her, breathing heavily.

"Why did you do it?" he said, his voice low and angry, hands grasping the chair arms to either side of her.

Willow stared up at him, her mouth agape, then she swallowed and shook her head. "It was Acacia's idea..."

"*What* was her idea?"

"That... that..."

"Spit it out," he shouted and shook the chair, causing Willow to let out a screech.

"We sent a message to that beast you've been shacking up with and told him you decided to stay here," Acacia replied, her voice calm.

"*Mother!*" Peggy said, aghast.

"Why would he believe you?" Juniper said as he stared daggers at her, then at Willow, fury making his voice hoarse.

"Be... because... I used the"—Willow grimaced and gestured feebly—"thing to disguise... um, my voice."

"The voice modulator?" Juniper replied, dumbfounded. "Wait... You *impersonated* me?"

"It's for the best, Juniper," Acacia said quietly. "I had the family name to think of... and you owe us."

"Owe... you?"

"For seventeen years of taking care of our father. For seventeen years of this house falling down around our ears. For seventeen years of having to cut corners and go without."

"It's not my fault that the colony ship disappeared!" Juniper growled, releasing Willow's chair. "I left here so I could make a better life for you... you spoiled, selfish, ungrateful *witch*."

"Well, you didn't. And now you have a chance to make things right."

"What? You're insane. Why would I do *anything* for you after this?" He stared at her, incredulous.

"Acacia just means... oh, Juny... you'd be better off *here*. You can help around the house like you've been doing. And you're young still... and just as pretty as you were the day you left. Do you have any idea what kind of looks you get from everyone? My god, even the doctor at the clinic... He was looking at you like he wanted to take a bite out of you," Willow said gently. "Imagine... a doctor! You'll never need for anything again."

Juniper let out a laugh that sounded hysterical even to his own ears, and he shook his head in disbelief. "I'm leaving," he said. "This afternoon. I'm done here."

"Juniper!" Acacia said sternly as she rose from her seat. "If you leave, you'll no longer be welcome here."

"*Welcome?*" Juniper said, laughing shrilly again. "Like you *welcomed* me this time?"

"You can't possibly go back to that... that... *monster*," Acacia tried when she realized the emptiness of her threat.

"The only monster I see here is you." And with that, Juniper left the room.

CHAPTER 15
WALKING INTO A DREAM

J uniper was dancing from foot to foot, impatient for the
Blackskimmer to finish docking with the *Stellerion*. It had
taken nearly a week and the last of his credits to get to the
big Chato-class ship—finding it had been a complete
gamble.

Marrex had picked up the damaged shuttlecraft in Frex
Symio Frex Ha, within the aBi nebula, so that's where Juniper
decided to look... and sure enough, they'd found the *Stellerion* in
a decaying orbit around a dead planet. No one had answered
their hails, but Juniper's gut told him that Marrex was indeed
aboard.

Finally, the hard dock was complete and the seal was
airtight. Juniper picked up his bag and turned to the men
standing outside the transfer passage. "Thank you," he said. "I
really appreciate the lift."

"You're welcome," replied the captain, showing his silver
baleen in the Krem version of a smile. "If you don't find this
Marrex, you could always come back and work for me." Only
one of his eyes were pointed at Juniper's face. The other four
were sweeping over his body for one last lingering look.

"I'll do that, Baran," Juniper replied, giving him a politely flirtatious smile. "Take care of yourselves." He nodded to the rest of the crew and walked through the hatch.

As soon as the interior door opened, Juniper closed his eyes and took a deep breath. The *Stellerion* even smelled like home to him. "S1N? VAL? Anyone?" he said as he stepped over the threshold. Behind him, the docking mechanism let out a hiss as the Blackskimmer's hatch closed.

Suddenly, two bright white spheres appeared in front of him. "Welcome, traveller," said the first sphere, the light dimming to the rhythm of its robotic speech.

Juniper frowned. "Uh. Thank you?"

"Please state which planetary government you represent," said the second sphere just as lifelessly as the first.

"None," Juniper replied. "Who are you? Where are S1N and VAL?"

"I am 2W-S1N, the ship's navigation system," the first answered.

"I am VAL-900. My primary function is life support aboard the *Stellerion*," said the second. "Would you like to learn more?"

Horrified, Juniper stared at the two AIs—Marrex had finally erased them just like he had always threatened to. For a moment, Juniper couldn't speak. It was like losing two of his best friends. Jaw clenched, he took a few breaths, angry and heartbroken. *Maybe there's a backup.*

"I just need to find the captain," he said, walking quickly down the hallway towards Marrex's garden. The two AIs kept in step with him, floating to either side.

"The captain has perished," said the one to his right. "Would you like to learn more?"

Juniper stopped in his tracks, the news like a punch to the stomach. He was too late. "No... no... he can't be dead." He shook his head. "No, I refuse to believe it."

"The captain has perished," repeated the orb.

"Shut up," Juniper growled.

He ran the rest of the way to the garden.

JUNIPER WAVED the door open and stepped inside, eyes wide. It was dark within, but by the light of the twin AI spheres, he could see the garden was in ruins. It looked as though someone had slashed trees and ripped up bushes, and the grass was torn up in great swaths. Taking the shortest path to the centre, Juniper found he had to wade through the babbling brook because the quaint little bridge was in pieces.

With every step, he whispered, "Please."

Finally, he reached the centre of the garden, and there, lying naked at the base of the statue, was Marrex. "No," he gasped, sinking to his knees beside the prone Ghelyxian. "Oh god... Marrex." Juniper extended a trembling hand and touched Marrex's bare back.

He frowned. The Ghelyxian's body was still warm... and *breathing*.

"Marrex?" he said, shaking the captain's shoulder.

Marrex let out a low mournful groan and turned his head, his eyes closed.

"Marrex!" Juniper said a little louder, giving him a more vigorous shake. "Wake up."

Slowly, Marrex's lids lifted, and he stared at Juniper, his expression of profound bemusement.

"What are you *doing*?" Juniper asked.

"I'm waiting to die," Marrex said, his voice a low grumble. "And now I'm dreaming of my Juniper."

Now that he knew Marrex was alive and apparently unscathed by the looks of him, Juniper's anguish made way for something closer to anger. "What the *hell* did you do to S1N and VAL? I hope to god you made a backup. And stop fucking looking at me like that. You're not dreaming, you fucking asshole. Shit! I've been gone three fucking weeks, you big, stupid—" Juniper said, punctuating is words with hard shoves that made Marrex wince and struggle into a sitting position "—fucking *idiot*. Why would you make me think you were in trouble or *dead*? What is *wrong* with you?"

"Is it... really you?"

"Of *course* it is..."

"You called and said you weren't going to return," Marrex said hoarsely.

"My *sisters* made that call before they sabotaged my communicator. *Why* would you believe it? It probably didn't even *sound* like me... it's not even a good voice modulator! *Why* the fuck would you just blindly accept what they said? Do you have so little faith in me? You weren't even just a *little* suspicious? Hm? Didn't you think to question them? See if it was really me? I *said* I was going to be back!" Juniper shouted and then burst into tears.

"Why are you crying?" Marrex asked, his eyes wide.

"Because, you ass, I don't know what I want to do more: punch you or kiss you," Juniper said through clenched teeth, the tears hot on his cheeks. "I flew across the damn galaxy, desperate to find you, and I'm *exhausted* from spending a week fending off a Blackskimmer captain who just could *not* keep his hands to himself, and I am furious that you would just gi-give up..." He wiped his nose and hiccupped a sob, his tirade petering out. "Why would you give up on me?" he asked in a small voice.

Marrex shook his head slowly, reaching to pull Juniper into his embrace. "I'm sorry," the Ghelyxian replied, holding him tight against his solid, furry chest.

"Was it really so hard for you to believe that I would come back to you?"

For a moment, Marrex said nothing, then he sighed. "I'm sorry."

Juniper looked up into the captain's face. Ghelyxians

couldn't cry, but Marrex looked as if he'd prove the biology texts wrong at any second. "Maybe you didn't realize something... something I guess I've only just figured out for myself," Juniper said.

The captain's black eyes searched his. "What is it?"

"I'm in love with you."

A few seconds passed, Marrex's nostrils flaring with his quick breaths, and then he leaned forward and kissed Juniper's lips softly. With a quiet moan, Juniper melted into the kiss, weak with relief and astounded by the profound ache in his heart. He thought he would start crying again—instead, he poured all of it into the passion of their kiss.

It was promise and conciliation, a union of body and soul unto itself, and as they grasped at each other in a fervour, nestled at the heart of the ruined garden, Juniper finally understood what it was that writers from time immemorial had striven to describe... How could anyone hope to capture something so overwhelming and fathomless?

Heart pounding, Juniper pulled back. "Lie back," he said, breathing heavily. "I want you."

Marrex's eyes widened, and then his nose wrinkled in a smile. "Are you certain this time?" he asked.

Juniper let out a laugh, surprised at the gentle teasing. "Yes. I'm absolutely certain this time."

MARREX GROANED and pushed his hips up, trying not to hurt Juniper but so aroused it was nearly impossible not to move. Fireflies sparked and danced around them in the darkened garden as Juniper rode Marrex slowly, his chest gleaming with sweat and his lips parted in a harsh, gasping pant—he whimpered, threw his head back, and yelled as a few weak drops fell from his limp cock into the mess in Marrex's belly fur.

Tears rolled down Juniper's cheeks as he shook his head, but he kept rising up on his knees and lowering again, sliding Marrex deep, as if in a trance and unable to stop himself. Shuddering, Juniper let out a desperate sob, his cock spitting out a single, pitiful drop, and Marrex shut his eyes, groaning at the way Juniper's heat squeezed him tight—he was teetering dangerously close to the edge himself.

Panting, Marrex slid his hands under Juniper's backside to support his weight, giving the exhausted Human some respite while slowing him further. Juniper groaned and came again, and this time Marrex wasn't able to delay his climax. He grunted, pulling Juniper down hard enough that he cried out weakly as Marrex pumped his seed into him, each pulse accompanied by a burst of such intense pleasure that Marrex was left a moaning, twitching mess in its wake.

Before Marrex could pull out, Juniper went down into the depths of yet another powerful orgasm, shaking so hard Marrex was afraid he'd pass out. He quickly lifted Juniper off, and drew him against his shoulder, hugging him tight and soothing him until the stimulant had run its course and Juniper was able to draw a breath without crying out.

"Wow... I... missed... that..." Juniper said when he could speak, a dazed smile on his face as he panted. His hair was drenched, sticking to his forehead and cheeks, and his eyes were heavy-lidded in a face that was flushed purple in the dark.

Marrex chuckled and nodded. "I missed *you*."

"But, Marrex, you have to promise me, swear to god, that you're never going to pull that kind of stunt again—there's *missing* me and then there's freaking the fuck out the way you did. Talk about melodramatic..."

"I'm sorry," Marrex said again, ashamed of how he'd acted. "I promise." Then he wrinkled his brow. "It's just... when you left, I could feel the changes starting again—the curse coming back."

Juniper shook his head. "You're crazy. You look fine... a little dirty, but no different from when I left."

"I don't?" Marrex asked, surprised. He touched the side of his head. "My horns... feel *here.*"

Juniper carefully investigated Marrex's head and shrugged. "I don't feel anything. I think it's probably just part of your *insane* overreaction, you big idiot."

Snorting, Marrex stared at Juniper, wondering why it felt so nice to be called an idiot by the young man. Maybe because it was said with such affection. The beautiful smile certainly helped.

"What I *don't* get is why those things said you were dead," Juniper said.

"What things?"

"You know... the not-S1N, not-VAL, floating nightlights?"

"The ship's AIs?" Marrex said, confused. "I told them no such thing." He cleared his throat and called out, "Computer."

Immediately, two white globes appeared before them. "What did you tell the Human?"

"It asked to see the captain. The captain is deceased," replied the sphere on the right.

"The captain has perished."

"Who is the captain?" Marrex asked them.

"Captain Jennock Hassim," they said in unison.

"Ah." Marrex nodded, catching on. "I reformatted the computer using an old memory crystal I found," he said to Juniper. "Captain Hassim was captain of the *Stellerion* before I took over. The AIs wouldn't assist me with anything until I told them the captain was dead..." He slowly trailed off, astonished by the look on Juniper's face. The young man was scowling at him. "What?"

"Please tell me you can bring S1N and VAL back," Juniper said, his voice low. "Just like they were before."

"I can," Marrex said quickly. Juniper had been fond of them

and, in truth, so had he. "They never gave up on you, Juniper. I should have listened to them, but I was too devastated to hear reason. They're safely stored in a backup crystal. Promise."

"Good." Juniper lay back down, carding his fingers through Marrex's chest fur. "All right... you're forgiven."

Marrex closed his eyes, enjoying Juniper's touch, and sighed. He *had* been a big idiot. After a while, Juniper's silence worried him. He lifted his head to look down at him.

The smile Juniper gave him was apprehensive.

"What is it?" Marrex asked, concerned.

Frowning, Juniper nibbled on the corner of his bottom lip as though he was reticent to speak. At long last he said, "Marrex, are you sure you really want *me*?"

"Of course. That's an absurd question."

"Is it?"

"Absolutely." Marrex laid his head back down on the springy moss grass and watched the fireflies above them, slowly caressing Juniper's smooth flank. "You stepped into my nightmare and transformed it into an enchanting dream... one I've been waiting for my whole life, it seems. Do you know what it means to me that you'd stay by my side and give your love to me?"

"What's that?" Juniper spoke in a hush, his voice tender.

"I never need wake from the dream."

144

EPILOGUE – 3 MONTHS LATER

Juniper walked down the hall, carrying a mug of hot chocolate in each hand. By his side hopped a large fluffy black rabbit.

"This is the stupidest mode of transportation," groused S1N, his ears flopping with every bounce. "Please change me back? I'm dying here."

"I think you're cute," Juniper said with a smirk. "And I'll change you back when I think you've suffered enough. You were downright *rude* to those Denobians."

"They left a mess in the dining hall! You should have seen the slime everywhere."

"I did, and that's no excuse to be such a dick. Do you have any idea how much profit we're making because of them? Their synaptic lubricant is the best on the market, and we're getting it at cost, S1N."

"Fine. I'm sorry," replied S1N, hopping along like an angry little storm cloud made of fluff. "Change me now?"

"Not yet."

Juniper stopped in front of a door. "VAL, can you let me in?" Immediately, the door slid open and he stepped inside, smiling.

Marrex looked up from the book he was reading, his brow wrinkled. "Is that hot chocolate?"

"It is."

"With *sheppik* crumbs in it?"

"Just like you like it," Juniper replied with a laugh, handing over the mug. He looked down at his father lying in bed with his eyes closed. He seemed so frail. Reaching out, Juniper took his father's limp hand and sat down on the other chair. "How is he?"

"I think he likes this better than the book of Ghelyxian poetry."

"No kidding," Juniper said. "What are you reading to him now?"

"It's called *Prince Marcassin*."

"How can you tell if he likes it?"

"I don't know... something changes in his face," Marrex replied, taking a sip of his hot chocolate. His nose wrinkled with pleasure. "Thank you for this, love. My throat was getting dry."

"You're very welcome." Juniper sighed and shook his head. "You know you don't have to read to him *every* day."

"I enjoy it. Besides, he's family now." Marrex looked down at his father-in-law. "I want him to know my voice."

Blinking quickly to dry his eyes, Juniper cleared his throat. "Speaking of family... I didn't know when the right time to tell you was..."

Marrex glanced up, his black eyes round. "Tell me what?"

Juniper fished in his pocket and pulled out an intricately folded piece of molimfibre. He stared down at it. The seal was broken, and the edges of the thin, flexible metal were creased from the half-dozen times he'd read through the short message.

Brow wrinkled, Marrex looked at the letter. "That's... a royal missive from Ghelyx." His black tongue darted out to lick his upper lip, a nervous gesture. "I don't understand."

"I... wrote to your cousin," Juniper said a little nervously.

146

"Why would you do that?" Marrex sounded like his old cantankerous self, and Juniper winced.

"I knew you'd freak out, which is why I was waiting for the perfect time... but I think you should really read this," Juniper said, unfolding the letter. He held it out to Marrex.

Marrex flared his nostrils, his shoulders hunching defensively, but he set aside his mug and took the letter, reading through it twice before sitting back in his seat. His pupilless eyes lifted to Juniper's.

"I don't understand," he repeated. "The letter is an invitation to meet her at the border of Imperial space."

"She's a *reformist*, Marrex. And she's going to be queen one day... probably soon."

Marrex let out a harsh laugh, shaking his head. "That means little."

"Does it? Besides, what can it hurt? She's agreed to meet you, and, once she sees you've changed so much, maybe she'll question this insane practice of exiling the cursed—maybe even push for that childhood treatment. You *can't* be the only Ghelyxian to experience some reversal of the condition."

Marrex looked back down at the letter, the muscles working in his jaw as he mulled over Juniper's words. Finally, he shrugged and grimaced. "There's reform... and then there is revolution. Things move slowly for my people." Juniper took a breath, set to argue further, but Marrex quickly put a hand over his mouth. "I wasn't saying no. I was just stating a fact." He cupped Juniper's chin, his thumb pressing against Juniper's lips gently. "I'll meet with her. Thank you."

"I'm sorry to interrupt," VAL broke in. His smooth face was the colour of a ripe peach, clashing wildly with the bright-green bow tie that floated beneath. Juniper thought the addition suited him quite well. "There is a shipment of belemedermidian clorex arriving shortly, and I was wondering where you would like it."

"Oh right," Juniper said. Reviving his father's company was proving to be more work than he'd expected. They were filling a much-needed trade role between legitimate businesses existing outside Imperial space and those within. It wouldn't be long before they'd have to hire more workers. "Tell Peggy to put them with the boxes of fetrenium ore."

Suffering from heartbreak over being dumped by her Cebari boyfriend, Peggy had been only too happy to spend her summer interning aboard the *Stellerion*. He'd never be on great terms with his sisters, especially Acacia, but he could be civil if it meant he could be part of his niece's life. Already, she was proving herself to be a great addition to the crew.

"Yes, Juniper," said VAL, his bow tie drifting a little further away and acquiring pink stripes as his face shifted to yellow. "I'll tell Peggy to put them with the fetrenium."

"No... not... fetrenium."

Startled, Juniper looked over at his father. The man still had his eyes closed, but his head moved weakly from side to side. "Dad?" He could barely breathe, thinking he'd imagined his father talking, but the pale lips parted, and his dad spoke again in a voice hoarse from disuse. "Not... fetrenium."

"What does it mean?" Marrex asked quietly.

"I have... no idea. Dad? Can you hear me?"

S1N rose up into the air, his bunny-nose twitching. "Scans show... hmm..."

"What is it?" Juniper slid his hand into Marrex's, and the Ghelyxian squeezed it gently.

"I'll tell you if you change me back."

"S1N!"

"Fine," replied the AI, sitting up midair, one ear up and the other down. "My scans show improved brain activity with a spike in key areas pertaining to memory processing and self-awareness."

"Not... next... fetrenium," muttered his father, shaking his head again.

"Dad?"

"Fetrenium... interacts... clorex." Gradually, his father's eyelids lifted, and he frowned at Juniper.

"Oh my god... Dad! Are you ok?" Juniper exclaimed, quickly taking both of his hands. "I was so worried."

"Fetrenium... BDM clorex... ore... clorex..."

His father's eyes lost their focus, and Juniper shook him lightly, trying to snap him out of it. "Dad?" he said, perturbed. He got no answer.

"He's been unresponsive for so long... I don't want you to get your hopes up, Juniper," Marrex said quietly. "It might just be a reflex... like muscle memory."

It was a bitter pill to swallow, but Juniper knew the Ghelyxian was just being logical. "I know. I'm just... let me be excited, all right?"

"Sorry." Marrex wrapped an arm around Juniper's waist, bestowing a kiss on the back of his head.

"Your old man's right, though," S1N announced. "I just looked it up—the two shouldn't be stored in the same vicinity. Airborne chemical traces of the ore could render the clorex inert should they mix. He certainly knows his business."

"Ok, Dad," Juniper said, smiling. He wiped a tear from his cheek. "I won't store them together. Thank you for the advice." He cleared his throat, trying to get rid of the lump. "VAL?"

"I'll relay the message," the AI said and winked out.

Slowly, his father's eyes closed. He seemed fast asleep.

"Well, at least it's a change," Juniper said, turning around to look up at Marrex. "And I'm happy, no matter how small it is."

"I am too," Marrex replied with a nod. He stroked a hand down Juniper's back, pulling him away from the bed. "Why don't we go finish that movie. I want to know what happens with Mr. Darcy and—"

"Juniper."

They both started and turned. His dad's eyes were open again, his gaze remarkably steady. "Good... choice... with... Marrex," he said, in his hoarse voice. Then he smiled, closed his eyes, and began to snore.

"I'd say that was more than just a reflex," Juniper said, laughing with giddy relief.

Marrex hugged Juniper to his chest. "Maybe there's a happily ever after in store for everyone in the end," he said in a low voice. "Come, let's leave him to sleep."

Looking back at his fluffy little tail, S1N wrinkled his nose in disgust. "Happily ever after? Yeah right."

VAL smiled wide. "I think it makes you look sweet and likeable... just like you truly are, even though you try to appear disinterested."

S1N lifted his head, staring at his counterpart. "Sweet?" he said faintly.

"Yes."

"And... likeable?"

"Very much so."

S1N blinked at VAL. "That bow tie makes you look stupid." His nose quivered uncontrollably as he looked away.

"You're welcome."

BOOKS BY BEY DECKARD

FOR AN UP-TO-DATE LIST OF TITLES, VISIT:

https://beydeckard.com/blog/buy-my-books/

MAX, THE SERIES

Max

Max, the Sequel

BAAL'S HEART SERIES

Caged: Love and Treachery on the High Seas

Sacrificed: Heart Beyond the Spires

Fated: Blood and Redemption

Careened: Winter Solstice in Madierus

F.I.S.T.S

Sarge

Murphy

F.I.S.T.S. Handbook For Individual Survival in Hostile Environments

THE ACTOR'S CIRCLE

The Complications of T

The Last Nights of The Frangipani Hotel

THE STONEWATCHERS

Kestrel's Talon

STANDALONE BOOKS

Better the Devil You Know

Exposed

Beauty and His Beast

The Blacksmith's Apprentice

SHORT STORIES

Don't Touch Me (UnCommon Bodies Anthology)

Rakka Surprise (UnCommon Lands Anthology)

About the Author

Artist, Writer, Dog Lover

Bey Deckard is the author of a number of novels including the *Baal's Heart books, Max, Beauty and His Beast,* and *Better the Devil You Know.*

Bey lives in Montréal, Canada where he spends most of his time writing, doing graphic work, painting portraits, speaking French, cooking tasty vegetarian eats, or watching more movies than is good for him. If you're the curious type, www.beydeckard.com is where you'll find art and free stories by Bey as well as information on his published works.

bey.deckard@gmail.com
Look for Deckard's Diablerie on Facebook

facebook.com/authorbeydeckard

twitter.com/BeyDeckard

instagram.com/beydeckard

goodreads.com/beydeckard

bookbub.com/authors/bey-deckard

www.ingramcontent.com/pod-product-compliance
Lightning Source LLC
Chambersburg PA
CBHW020417150626
46554CB00014B/1893